Praise for *R*

"A 16-year-old girl detective stars in a mystery paying tribute to Sherlock Holmes... This series opener is pleasurably packed with clever, solvable, well-explained puzzles; hits the spot for a mystery lover."

Kirkus Reviews

"First-time novelist Chesterman creates an engrossing story that keeps readers chasing the truth. ... Fans of quirky protagonists, puzzling mysteries, and spy craft will enjoy this."

School Library Journal

"It was intoxicating to have such a strong character use intellect rather than supernatural abilities or weaponry to solve the minor puzzles (where the reader is pitted against Arcadia) and the more sinister mystery twists that ultimately shake Arcadia's trust in family and identity."

Glee Books

I, Huckleberry

a novel

Simon Chesterman

With the support of

Published by Marshall Cavendish Editions
An imprint of Marshall Cavendish International

Other Marshall Cavendish Offices:
Marshall Cavendish Corporation, 800 Westchester Ave, Suite N-641, Rye Brook, NY 10573, USA • Marshall Cavendish International (Thailand) Co Ltd, 253 Asoke, 16th Floor, Sukhumvit 21 Road, Klongtoey Nua, Wattana, Bangkok 10110, Thailand • Marshall Cavendish (Malaysia) Sdn Bhd, Times Subang, Lot 46, Subang Hi-Tech Industrial Park, Batu Tiga, 40000 Shah Alam, Selangor Darul Ehsan, Malaysia

Marshall Cavendish is a registered trademark of Times Publishing Limited

National Library Board, Singapore Cataloguing in Publication Data

Name(s): Chesterman, Simon.
Title: I, Huckleberry : a novel / by Simon Chesterman.
Description: Singapore : Marshall Cavendish Editions, [2020]
Identifier(s): OCN 1152340336 | ISBN 978-981-48-6896-9 (paperback)
Subject(s): LCSH: Teenagers--Fiction. | Mental health--Fiction. | Teenagers--
Mental health--Fiction. |
Classification: DDC 828.99343--dc23

Printed in Singapore

For T

The mind is its own place, and in itself
Can make a heav'n of hell, a hell of heav'n.

John Milton, *Paradise Lost*

Part One

Now

Is it all right if we don't begin at the beginning? To make sense of things, to really understand, you sometimes have to start at the end. Time's funny like that. We experience life in one direction—a series of moments and encounters, flowing one to the next. Yet their significance only dawns on us as our own sun begins to set.

It's a cliché that youth is wasted on the young. That kind of misses the point. Youth is all potential: everything's possible. If we knew what was coming, if we could foresee the doors that would open and those that would slam in our faces, then who would bother? The daily struggles that loom like mountains, then recede in the rear-view mirror. When you're a kid, every day is a new beginning. Even the police give us a free pass, wiping the slate clean at the magical age of eighteen. A chance to start over. By then, though, it's too late. You are who you were. One day you look back and every step that you thought was a choice seems predestined, nudging you, pushing you to wherever the hell you ended up. Every decision, every happenstance, inexorably forming your character and shaping your destiny.

In any case, to make sense of my story you definitely need to begin with the end. We'll get to the only child, born-to-loving-parents-in-Riverdale, NY, and so on soon. None of that means anything unless you know where it is leading. Which is to me, age sixteen, running up the stairs of a medieval clock tower, clutching a fragment of an 800-year-old parchment, booted footsteps clattering behind me.

The banister is slick and offers neither balance nor grip. I reach another wooden landing and pause to catch my breath, panting clouds of vapour into the cold night air. The wood creaks under my weight—too many kebabs, I guess. With enough force it might be possible to smash some of the beams, but that's unlikely to block the path. In my pocket, my fingers close on Kat's cigarette lighter. A fire? But the wood is too damp.

The footsteps below do not pause. Onward and upward, then. I continue to climb, one leg after the other, though that's as far ahead as my plan goes. The parchment is getting damp. In the bare light of the stairwell I imagine the text beginning to bleed, quill strokes of a thirteenth-century royal scribe undone by a twenty-first-century dropout.

And criminal. If only it were the police chasing me. The boots reach another landing and continue up the next flight. My leg aches but I push on, past the frozen mechanism of the clock, bursting suddenly through an arch and onto a narrow balcony, its crenellated ledge overlooking spires and gabled roofs. The mist has become a drizzle and I almost slip on the weatherworn stone. I take out my phone, but it's too late. Thirteen messages. Nowhere else to run and no one left to call.

From the street below, student carollers rouse themselves against the rain once more and break into song. They probably stand around a cardboard box or open violin case, raising money for starving children, animal welfare, some worthy cause. What they lack in talent they make up for in enthusiasm. Bless them. Urgent good tidings and dreams of figgy pudding waft up from the cobbled street below. It almost brings a smile.

Almost. I wonder what hitting the cobblestones from this height will feel like. Painful, most likely, before the darkness. The footsteps behind me slow as they approach the archway, wary of a trap. I turn my back, looking out across the dreaming spires one last time. The still night air carries the voices of the carollers, offering final wishes for a Merry Christmas. Until the resonance is broken by the scrape of a knife on stone, whetting the blade one last time before the end.

She fooled us all. My fingers tighten on the parchment, damp ink now leeching through to my skin. I close my eyes and brace myself for what is to come.

Then

1

So, I was indeed born to loving parents in Riverdale, New York. Technically, that's the Bronx, but our neighbourhood had more in common with the Upper West Side than the rest of the borough. Going by property prices and school fees, we might as well have been part of gentrified Manhattan. Even the numbered streets just carried on into the two hundreds, after a small gap that appears to have sunk in Spuyten Duyvil Creek.

My parents were academics who met as New Yorkers studying abroad at Oxford University. Maybe that fixed its place for them as a kind of romantic time capsule, idealised for architecture and academia as much as for the fading memory of their own youth. A photograph of the two of them in a convertible hung in our hallway, green hills rolling behind their younger and happier selves. They gave up driving years ago and now rarely look beyond the city. I remember Dad explaining the sun's motion by saying that it rises in the Upper East Side and sets in the Upper West

Side. It was years later that I found out he stole that from a *New Yorker* cartoon.

I say my parents were loving, but they weren't exactly affectionate. Our bookshelves bore dozens of tomes on developmental neurobiology, child psychology, and so on, mostly purchased in the three months leading up to my birth. I was a teenager before I began to understand that my parents were more comfortable thinking of me as a challenging new research project than the fruit of their loins.

Mom and Dad's hearts were usually in the right place, but their methods left something to be desired. As part of a war on sugar when I was eight, Mom spent several weeks trying to persuade me that the ice cream cart occasionally plying our streets only rang its bell when it had run out of ice cream. A falsifiable claim, as I showed her in chocolate mint. She was angry but took a photo nonetheless. I still have it somewhere.

Another of their obsessions was the danger posed by social media. When they finally consented to let me have my own phone at age twelve—a few well-placed news articles about kidnappings may have helped my case—they bought the only device still in production that had no access to the internet. That put me in the niche market that lumped the children of over-protective parents together with old folks who just wanted a damn telephone with numbers like they used to make.

Oh, and they named me Huckleberry. As Dad never tired of explaining, this was after Mark Twain's most famous character, who rafted down the Mississippi River in the antebellum South with an escaped slave on a crusade against racism. "What will be your crusade, son?" he used to ask. When I got around to reading *Huckleberry Finn*, I pointed out to him that Huck only ended up on the river because his father was the town drunk—and that he thought he would go to hell for freeing Jim.

Dad looked fit to explode—he wasn't big on being contradicted—but Mom told me she liked the name precisely because Huck did the right thing, despite what everyone else believed. "A good heart is a better guide in this world than a badly trained conscience," she told me. "Aim for that, and you'll do just fine."

Mrs Sellwood used to say that wisdom is the compliment that experience pays to failure. She said a lot of stuff. Much of it sounded like it came off the side of a cereal box, but every now and then she cut through the BS and helped me see something true and real. She never commented on my name, except once she asked me if I was going to let my name define me, or if I was going to define it. At the time, I said I wasn't sure. Maybe I am now.

Despite the all-American name, or maybe because of it, I inherited Mom and Dad's fascination with England. Alongside the how-to books on child development were books on King Arthur, Stonehenge, and Jack the Ripper. To these I added countless variations on the English boarding school novel, dreaming that my parents might send me off in top hat and tails to attend Eton or the like. That never happened, but as my sixteenth birthday approached they mentioned over dinner that they'd enrolled me in a winter programme at Oxford.

By then a new pile of books was growing, on the topic of college admissions—the next module in my parents' Child-Rearing 101. It was pretty clear that a December in England was meant to plant a seed about doing university there, or maybe it was CV-padding for applications back home. Mom was upbeat as usual, telling me how much fun I would have. Vague on details, though. As for Dad, he got this exasperated look when I asked him why this was sprung on me so suddenly. "It'll be good for you," was all he said, as if I was still in a high chair and he was shovelling broccoli into my mouth.

Personally, I was pretty confident I could get into Harvard or Yale if I wanted to. A line mentioning Oxford on the application wouldn't hurt. Brand name colleges like brand name students.

Well, let's back up a step. It might be an exaggeration to say that I was on a path to waltz into Harvard or Yale. My grades were good but not stratospheric. I had the usual cello-debating-public service record, but was hardly Nobel Prize material.

Truth be told, I struggled a bit. My grades were above average, sure. Though this was at a school where half the students were there to learn how to manage the income from their trust funds. And I was never on the debate team. I don't know why I said that I was—it sort of rolled off the tongue and onto the page. I did argue with my teachers, I suppose. But you don't normally—*one* does not normally put that on one's curriculum vitae.

It was Mrs Sellwood who had first encouraged me to think about going abroad. Unlike most of my teachers, she seemed to want to understand me rather than just get through the day. She also knew I was interested in psychology and mentioned once that the programme at Oxford was first-rate. Some time away from the US wouldn't hurt either. "As a girl," she told me, "I spent a year in Australia with relatives. In that time, I learned something about that country, and I learned a great deal about my home by seeing it from a distance. But most of all I learned about myself."

So Mom talked school into letting me out a few weeks early, and off to England it was. I waved so long to Felix and the trust-fund bunch, packed my brolly (that's an umbrella), and we arrived in Oxford one glorious day on the bus from Heathrow Airport. Blue sky and sunlight made the limestone buildings glow; secret college lawns and neighbouring fields shone the purest green. We walked the cobblestone streets, Mom and Dad giggling at memories they were too embarrassed to share with me.

Until the clouds returned and a veil of drizzle marked the onset of winter. Even so, any deficiencies in the English climate were more than compensated for by the English people themselves. Mom and Dad had briefed me on how to avoid being an ugly American abroad, but nothing could prepare me for the English. They were even more polite than Canadians. After Mom and Dad went back to their hotel, I saw an old man hit his head on a door and the first thing to come out of his mouth was, "Sorry."

I had to stop and write that one down in my diary straight away. A gift from Mom, it was bound in dark green leather with crisp, creamy paper and faint grey lines. Fancier than my usual notebooks—standard black with red corners, 192 pages held together by an elastic closure—it took a little getting used to. But a new country meant turning over a new leaf figuratively, so why not also do it literally? Hah. I wrote that down also.

That was when I first saw Kat. Standing outside the college entrance, she was leaning against a stone column and staring into the middle distance as though she were posing for a portrait. In New York, I once went to the Met to see an exhibition of Pre-Raphaelite art. Kat reminded me of Proserpine—pale skin, raven hair, a hint of doom. I had just sat down on a bench to write when I smelled something burning. It took a moment to trace it to the cigarette held at her side. She brought it up to her lips, an orange glow followed by a lazy expulsion of smoke.

She realised that I was staring before I did. I looked away, but she was already moving in my direction. Finishing the sentence, my diary closed as a waft of nicotine and perfume preceded her.

"What's the matter," she said, a mix of challenge and curiosity in her voice. The top two buttons of a dark blue shirt were undone, revealing a birthmark on her neck. I tried not to stare at that either. "Haven't you seen someone smoke before?"

I stood up, blurting out the first thing that came into my head. Unfortunately, it was the truth. "Well, not anyone under forty," I said. "Don't you guys vape here?" I had got up too quickly and my left leg nearly gave way, remnant of a childhood injury. I tried not to wince.

"Oh, you're *American*," she laughed, smoke following

her words and drifting into my face. Her perfume recalled the duty-free shop at the airport, but the smoke was giving me a headache. "That explains a lot." She raised the diminishing cigarette to her lips once more, then looked at it in disappointment. Exhaling to the side this time, she dropped the butt on the ground, extinguishing it under the heel of a patent-leather pump.

"What exactly does it explain?"

She was already absorbed in her phone. "Luncheon. Must dash. Bye." She looked me briefly in the eye, contemplated smiling, thought better of it, swung a bag onto her shoulder, and disappeared into the college.

I watched her leave, then put the diary into my backpack. I waited before reaching in to take out a tissue. Kneeling, I picked up the cigarette butt. Flecked with a deep red from her lipstick, I held it at a distance until I could drop it in the trashcan—rubbish bin—by the door.

Her lunch appointment, I soon discovered, was the same one as mine: a welcome meal at our new home-away-from-home, Warneford. That morning, Mom and Dad had dropped me and my luggage off in the pokey new quarters assigned to me, before trying to walk off some of the jetlag.

Check-in had been more elaborate than the summer camp in Maine. Dad had to pull out his reading glasses to squint at page after page of agreements and waivers, signing my rights away with a flourish. A bored administrator presented me with a black wristband—some kind of low-end Fitbit, by the look of it—and then asked for a cheek swab and a strand of my hair.

"But we've only just met!" I joked.

Mom tittered, but the administrator's expression did not change. At last, I opened my mouth so that she could run a Q-tip down the inside and seal it in a plastic cylinder. She then produced a pair of blunt-looking scissors, so I yanked out a couple of hairs for her. They went into another cylinder.

"Welcome to Warneford," she intoned.

If I had teeth like that, I wouldn't smile much either. "Thanks," was all I said. Then I felt bad; the poor state of English dentistry wasn't her fault. Mrs Sellwood used to say that it took more muscles to scowl than to smile, and that this was nature's way of telling us to be nice to one another. I'm pretty sure that was bogus, but I thanked the lady again.

Mom and Dad walked me back to my room. I tried out the wristband, which unlocked the door.

"No need to worry about losing your keys," Mom said.

I tried the lock a few more times. "Why am I here again?" I asked.

"Oh for God's sake," Dad burst out. "We've been over this a dozen times."

Mom put her hand on his arm. "It's a camp for exceptional teenagers, bright boys and girls, like you. A chance to get to know them and, especially, to get to know yourself. Go in with an open mind, OK?"

"OK." I looked out the window at the bleak sky. "I still don't understand why we couldn't go skiing in Vermont."

Mom raised a finger to stop Dad's response. "Many of the kids here are interested in psychology, same as you," she said. "You'll have classes with some of the best people at Oxford. It's going to be great."

I fiddled with the wristband. "Mrs Sellwood did say that the programme here was one of the best."

The sound of Dad's hand slapping the wall made me jump. "Of all things, that's the one you can't leave behind."

Mom shot him a look. "Come on," she said. "Let's take a photo outside before Dad and I go back to the hotel. Then it's going to be time for your orientation programme. They said all scheduled activities will go straight into your calendar."

We went to the front entrance and asked an old man on his way inside to take our photo. I waved goodbye to Mom and Dad as the man hit his head on the door, apologising to it. I sat to write that down, met the cigarette-toting Proserpine, she left, and then my own phone buzzed—an iPhone, at last!—the calendar telling me to make my way to the dining hall for orientation.

I followed the signs down unfamiliar corridors. The main building dated from the early nineteenth century, but much of its interior had last been renovated in the 1960s, at peak linoleum. According to my parents, it was smaller than most of the other Oxford colleges and lacked their gothic grandeur, but the hall was cosy and welcoming.

The smell of roast beef greeted me as I entered. A pleasant-faced woman with better teeth and a clipboard ticked a box and directed me to table seven, where tent cards with our given names in a light san serif font had been arranged. Table seven consisted of myself and three others, including cigarette girl, whose name card said "Catherine", but that had been crossed out with a thick marker and "Kat" written in its place.

"Huckleberry?" She beamed at me, flicking a lock of dark hair from her cheek. "Seriously? That's your name? Well, do join us." She turned to our companions. "Please allow me to introduce you to"—she angled her head to read the other cards—"Mei and …" She frowned and then shrugged. "And this gentleman."

"Tshombe," he introduced himself, rising to shake my hand. "Think the first part of 'church' and the latter part of 'Bombay'."

"Actually, I think they prefer it to be called 'Mumbai' now," said the other girl at our table, pushing a pair of rimless glasses back up the bridge of her nose. "Not that you," she hastily continued, "not that you need to change the way you pronounce your name." She closed her eyes for a full second, then opened them again as if entering the room for the first time. "I'm Mei," she said brightly, standing to shake hands. Like Kat and Tshombe, she wore the black wristband, though she kept it over the sleeve of her blouse.

"Huck," I replied. "Are you, like, Chinese? Your English is really good." Then it was my turn to cringe.

If she was offended, she did not show it. "I'm from Singapore. Your English isn't bad either, for an American."

Fair enough, I thought.

Tshombe straightened his tent card. "Don't worry," he grinned at me, reading my uncertainty. "I am indeed African—Zambian, to be precise. Huck, eh? Yes, that is better than Huckleberry. A nice strong name. And probably one that you do not need to spell out three times when you speak on the telephone."

Kat flicked her hair again. "Now, isn't this chummy. But where are my manners. You've all come from thousands of miles away and I've come from Basingstoke. I'm also the only Warneford veteran at the table, so I suppose that makes me your host. Come, then, let us feast on soggy potatoes, overdone roast beef, and peas boiled within an inch of their lives."

Other diners were heading toward a lunch counter and we joined the line—the queue. The other students wore wristbands also, holding them up to a sensor that issued a low beep before they collected their lunch.

"So, your parents are big Mark Twain fans?" Mei asked.

"Just pretentious," I replied, a little testily. "Plus, with a surname like Jones, my parents thought it would make me 'distinctive'."

"Huh," she said. "Sometimes I'm glad my name is so common. Sometimes it's nice to be anonymous. Maybe if your parents had named you Jacob you would have been happier." She squinted at the roast beef that was about to be dropped on her plate. "Excuse me," she addressed the server. "Is it possible to get a piece that's not entirely fat?" He looked at her blankly, the slice of meat landing on her plate with a slap. "Fine," she said under her breath. "I'll cut it off myself." She accepted some vegetables and returned to the table.

"So, American." Tshombe pounded me on the back. "What brings you here?"

Good question, I thought. Why the hell am I here? But I could hardly tell him that. "Oh, the same as everyone else. Also, I'm considering studying psychology one day."

"I see, yes." He nodded, and then shook his head. "But not the same as me. It was my father who brought me here. 'Time to grow up, son,' he said. 'Time to be a man.'" He sighed.

The server at the beef station put a piece of meat on each of our plates. Tshombe was a good head taller and probably thirty pounds heavier than me. He hesitated, plate in mid-air, and the server looked up at him, before placing a second slice of beef on his plate. A ladle duly drowned the beef in sauce, threatening to drip over the edge as he carried it across the hall.

When we returned to the table, Mei was pushing a small mound of peas around half a potato.

"Not hungry?" I asked.

"The cooks here seem more interested in punishing food than cooking it. I swear I can't taste anything." She reached into her bag and produced a small bottle with a red cap, tapping a few drops onto her beef.

"Is that Tabasco sauce?" I asked.

"I'm sorry, would you like some?" She offered the bottle to me. I shook my head, but Tshombe accepted it and sprayed some liberally on his beef. "Be careful," she observed. "It's a little hot."

"What about you, Huckleberry?" Kat inquired, reaching over to spear a piece of my carrot with her fork. "How do you find the cuisine?"

"My parents lived here twenty years ago, so I was warned about warm beer and lousy food."

She took another piece of carrot but paused when it was an inch from her lips. "So, what did attract you to England?"

On my left, Tshombe took a bite of his meat and coughed.

"I don't know." I tried the peas, most of which had been reduced to a green slime but tasted quite good if you avoided looking at them. "I always liked English history—King Arthur and all that. The rise and fall of Empire."

"You mean you find our fading status quaint?" Kat inquired, reddening slightly. She put the fork down on the table. "You like the fact that we're more comfortable reliving past glories than facing the future?"

"That's not what I said." I put my cutlery down also, hoping to avoid a scene.

Beside me, Tshombe was dabbing at his mouth and forehead with a handkerchief.

"She's only pretending to be irritated," Mei interjected through a mouthful of potato. "If you look at her eyes, you can tell that she's playing with you."

Kat gave Mei a curious look, evaluating her somehow. Then she picked up her fork and took a last stab at my carrots before addressing her own plate.

By this point, beads of sweat were appearing on Tshombe's brow and he drained the glass that was on the table before him.

Mei stood up. "I did warn you," she said. "Let me see if I can get you some milk." Tshombe smiled through watering eyes.

"Have you met the head of the programme yet?" Kat asked, the irritation washing from her face like a retreating wave.

"Professor Cholmondeley?" I said, pronouncing carefully

the name I had copied into my diary from the welcome note in my room.

Kat stared at me and then burst out laughing. It was a curiously high-pitched sound, equal parts jolly and mocking. "Chol-mon-de-ley," she mimicked, in a rough approximation of an American accent. "It's pronounced 'Chumley', doofus."

I had only ever seen the name in writing and there was no indication that half the letters had been added in a bid to trick the unwary. "And to think you English still complain about how Americans had to clean up the way you spell," I said, cutting a piece of beef and popping it in my mouth.

Well, that's not quite true. To be honest, what I said was "Oh." Then I cut the beef and ate it.

Mei returned with a small bowl of ice cream and placed it before Tshombe. "This should help."

He took a large spoonful into his mouth and sat back in relief. "Thank you," he whispered, a thin trail of melted vanilla running down his chin.

Kat leaned toward the centre of the table. "Let me fill you in on a little secret about our beloved director: Dr Cholmondeley was almost fired last year."

"For what?" Tshombe, fortified by the ice cream, had resumed his meal, painstakingly cutting pieces of beef not touched by the Tabasco sauce.

"Two students died," said Kat quietly. "The official version is that it was accidental, but there were lots of reasons to be suspicious."

"How did they die?" Mei asked, taking her seat.

Kat looked around the hall, as if reassuring herself that no one else was listening. "They fell. From the clock tower."

The tower was far older than the college itself, the remnant of a medieval church that had been incorporated into the nineteenth-century design. It rose above the rest of the buildings and was visible from miles away. When we arrived, we had been told that it was a site of some historic interest, but strictly off-limits to students as the structure was unsafe. No longer maintained, its hands were stuck permanently at eight minutes past eight.

"From your tone, you clearly don't believe that they fell on their own," Mei said. "Were they boys?"

"Why is that your first question?" Tshombe now seemed fully recovered.

"Statistically, men choose more violent methods for suicide," Mei replied. "Alternatively, two men are more likely to have been fighting or showing off and plunged to their deaths."

"It was a boy and a girl," Kat said. "And it was never clear what happened. One morning, the students arrived to find a police tent set up in the courtyard below the clock tower."

"So, why was Professor Cholmondeley—I'm sorry, *Chumley*—blamed for this?" I asked.

"She runs the camp and they were in her tutorial group." Kat lowered her voice even further, so that we all had to lean in to hear her. "She was the last person to see them before they died. The story is that she was arguing with them about something. Other students saw them outside her office. Cholmondeley said that the argument was about a disciplinary matter, that the boy had been drinking. The one part of the argument that other students overheard was the boy—Chester—yelling at Cholmondeley: 'You lied to us. This whole thing is a lie!'

"And then they were gone."

Kat concluded at a moment when other conversations in the hall had also paused, leaving the room silent but for the occasional scrape of fork on crockery. I looked around at the other tables, a dozen of which were set up like ours. Fifty or so students, from the looks of it drawn from around the world. As voices restarted, I picked up a couple of American accents and some Spanish. Surely, if the deaths had happened last year and there were returning students like Kat then there was no need to whisper?

Mei's brow crinkled and she was about to ask her own question when a rapping noise from the other end of the hall drew our attention. In addition to the tables of students, a longer table had been set up for the adults who presumably ran the programme. In comparison with the diversity of the students, the faces on that table were mostly pale. Mom's comment that the English sun took the colour *from* your cheeks came to mind.

A stout woman in her forties stood up. Around four and a half feet tall, her head barely rose above those of the students seated near her. She banged once more on a table with the heavy silver ring on her index finger.

"Professor Cholmondeley?" I mouthed at Kat, who nodded.

"Welcome, welcome," the professor bellowed. "It is my great honour to welcome you to the Warneford family. You come from all over the country and, indeed, all over the world. Here we shed those differences in the interests of growing as individuals, realising our potential, achieving our dreams."

Was this a camp about psychology or about leadership? The note in my room also went on about dreams, potential, and "holistic education". I looked at the faces of the other students, but it was the usual mix of attentiveness and boredom. A few fidgeted and a tall blond boy was playing some kind of drum solo on the table with his fingers.

"At Warneford," she continued, "we believe in holistic education. You will, I hope, learn much from my colleagues and me. But you will also learn from each other—as we will learn from each of you. At the same time, we aim to provide a supportive environment. If you need help, we are here." She nodded to the other adults sitting to her left and right, a few acknowledging her and looking around at the students also. "In my experience, however, it is often one's peers who first see signs of unhappiness. So, if you see a friend having a difficult time, perhaps not eating or sleeping as regularly as they should, please reach out to them. Ask how they are doing, if they need anything."

She paused, looking down. Was she thinking of the clock tower? "Such a helping hand can make all the difference."

A series of administrative announcements followed, essentially repeating information about mealtimes and curfews distributed on paper when we arrived. There was also a warning about staying away from the local pubs as a student from another college had apparently been stabbed during a fight. She concluded with yet another welcome to Warneford, which earned a polite round of applause.

Two more knocks of her ring on the table indicated the end of lunch. Students filed out of the hall, but she remained in place, bodies parting around her like a small rock in a shallow stream.

Then the rock began to move toward our table. Professor Cholmondeley nodded to Kat. "It's good to see you again, Miss Evershaw. Is everything in order?"

"Yes, Ma'am." Kat's head bowed as she said it.

"Aren't you going to introduce me to your friends?"

Kat looked at us. "This is Tshombe from Zambia, Mei from Singapore, and Huckleberry from New York."

"Why, what a little United Nations you have gathered together," said the professor, bringing her hands together and eyeing each of us in turn. "I do hope you will all be happy here and find whatever it is that you are looking for." Her eyes lingered on me. "I remember corresponding with Mrs Sellwood about you, Mr Jones. A fine woman. I am sorry that we didn't get a chance to meet." She looked at her watch. "Oh dear, I'm late for an appointment. See you in class, I suppose."

How did she know Mrs Sellwood? Professor Cholmondeley had a curious way of moving such that the upper part of her body remained still, gliding along while short legs propelled her forward. Less of a stone and more of a duck, I noted, as she paddled out of the hall, down a corridor, and out of sight.

Back in my room, I decided to send a quick email to Mrs Sellwood:

Dear Mrs Sellwood, I'm in Oxford! Sorry I didn't get to say goodbye before I left. I'll be sure to send you a photo of me punting once I figure out what that is. Professor Cholmondeley says she knows you. Small world!

Yours sincerely,
Huck

I hit send, but before closing the laptop a flashing envelope announced a new message in my inbox:

The e-mail address you entered could not be found. Please check the recipient's e-mail address and try to resend the message. If the problem continues, please contact your helpdesk.

I did check, and there was no mistake in the address. At the time, I assumed that Mrs Sellwood—who was something of a Luddite—had somehow misconfigured her email. At the time, I was wrong.

2

"You will not catch me."

"Trust me, Tshombe," I replied. "I will catch you."

"You will not be *able* to catch me," he insisted. "I am far heavier than you. I will knock you over, you will let go of me, and I will fall down and hit my head."

This was becoming tedious. "Trust me, Tshombe," I said again. "That's kind of the whole point."

Kat and Mei had completed their own trust falls and were watching us with amusement. Kat said that she had gone through all this last year and feigned boredom, but there were moments when her façade gave way to what seemed like happiness. Then she would look around, as if to make sure no one had seen it.

The second day of orientation covered basic information about life at Warneford and now focused on building camaraderie. This resembled other camps I had been to. Would we end up sitting around a fire toasting marshmallows and telling ghost stories? The English weather would probably make short shrift of that.

Our groups were the same as lunch the day before. Beside us, a pair of English boys with spiky hair argued about the European Union with a French girl, their Indian partner trying to mediate until Professor Cholmondeley intervened. Cooperative games and artistic challenges using found objects gave way to trust exercises. We had carried Mei, the lightest in our group, across an obstacle course and the final activity for the afternoon was falling backward into the arms of your partner.

"When I was eight years old," Tshombe said, looking over his shoulder at me, "my little sister and I shared a bunk bed. I slept on the top bunk, which you reached by climbing a ladder. One day, my father set me on the top bunk and said, 'Tshombe, jump—I will catch you.' I was very frightened of heights, but he kept saying, 'Jump, jump.' Finally, I agreed to jump into his arms. As I did, he stepped aside and let me crash to the floor. 'Never trust anyone,' he said. And then he walked out the door."

"Well that's messed up," I replied. "Why would he do such a thing?"

"My father has strange ways of showing his love," Tshombe said. "He hates softness, he hates weakness. We want for nothing at home, but we must strive for everything. I remember one day I broke a window with a ball. I apologised, but evidently it was not sincere enough. He accused me of thinking that I was better than everyone else. 'You think you are special?' he scolded me. 'You are not special. I can go with your mother and make another one like you tonight. No, you are not so special.'"

"He sounds like a real charmer," Kat said as she walked to stand before Tshombe. "Now, are you going to do your fall or wait until that bird above you craps on your head?"

Though we were indoors, Tshombe looked up to try to see this bird—at which point Kat stepped forward and pushed his chest firmly with both hands. A gasp of surprise escaped his lips as he fell back and into my arms. Unfortunately, the speed at which he moved and the fact that I looked up also meant I was unprepared; his weight caused me to lose my own balance and fall down, his body knocking the wind out of mine.

We lay on the ground as Kat pulled out her phone and took a picture. "Very elegant," she observed. "You two should try ballroom dancing."

When it was clear that neither of us was injured, we laughed. "At least," I said, "you didn't hit your head."

The organised activities soon concluded and we had an hour before dinner. Kat suggested going to a small café inside the college that sold pastries and a dark liquid that the man who worked there asserted, deadpan, was coffee. There was a Starbucks in town, but by now the drizzle had settled in and the local brew cost one tenth of a latte.

"I've decided to learn German," Kat declared as the four of us sat down. "It's a wonderful language—so earthy, so guttural. You know that all the simple words in English come from German, while the fancy ones come from French? The basic, boring 'green' comes from the German *Grün*, while the fancier 'verdant' comes from the French word for the same colour: *vert*."

I vaguely recalled an English teacher saying something

along these lines many years ago. Kat, I later learned, was prone to such impassioned conversions—picking up and dropping hobbies like a new favourite song.

"The best thing about German," she continued, "is that they have words that don't exist in English. Like that feeling you get when you take a sneaky pleasure in someone else's misfortune. I once actually saw someone slip on a banana peel—seriously, the funniest thing I have seen in my life. The Germans call it *Schadenfreude.* My personal favourite is *Backpfeifengesicht,* which is a word for something I didn't even realise I needed to be able to say: a person whose face is in need of a good slapping."

She looked at us each in turn and I half-expected her to slap someone, before she broke into a smile.

"You left out *Witzelsucht,*" Mei added. "It's a mental condition marked by poor jokes and the telling of pointless stories at which the speaker is intensely amused." She froze. "Not that that's what you were doing. Or suffer from." Again, she closed her eyes. I thought I saw her lips move—was she counting to three? "That all came out wrong," she said. "Anyway, who would like some more coffee?"

"I'll tell you what," Kat said. "Why don't we play another game." She gestured toward the table where a range of pastries was displayed. "Let's see who can steal three of those cupcakes. Get them off the tray without being asked to pay for them."

Mei's brow furrowed. "Why would I want to do that? The money raised at this café goes to charity. And if we get caught—"

"Fine," Kat interrupted her. "You can leave money

afterward if you like, and I promise to explain that it was an orientation activity if we get caught. But I challenge you to show that you *could* get away with swiping them in broad daylight."

Mei weighed this, fingers pulling at the end of her left sleeve. I think she knew she was being manipulated, but made the calculation that at least Kat had forgiven her for calling her jokes poor and her stories pointless. She nodded.

There were two workers in the café, the man behind the cash register pouring coffee and a teenage girl moving in and out of a small pantry to clear tables and wash dishes. Mei observed their movements for a full minute. Then, as the man welcomed a new customer and the girl took a pile of plates into the back, she rose and went over to the pastries, putting first one, then two, and then a third chocolate iced cupcake into her handbag and returning to sit down.

Her face was flushed, anxious but also excited. "I would never have done that in Singapore," she said breathlessly. Looking around, she added, "They should install CCTV here; it's far too easy to steal."

Tshombe had watched all this and now turned to Kat. "Come now, Miss Evershaw," he said. "Mei has lived up to her side of the bargain. I believe that you have some cakes to steal also?"

Kat raised an eyebrow. "Very well," she conceded. She stood and approached the cupcakes, but the man behind the register was unoccupied and saw her.

"Can I help you, dear?" he asked. I later learned that his name was Stephen.

Without batting an eyelid, Kat asked him, "Would you like to see a magic trick?"

He was in his late twenties, a graduate student, I assumed, working part-time at the café. "Not particularly," he demurred.

"Oh, come on," Kat oozed charm, touching him playfully on the sleeve. "Let me show you my magic trick?"

He crossed his arms. "All right. Show me."

Kat grinned. "OK, watch this." She took one of the chocolate iced cupcakes from the tray, holding it between finger and thumb, lifting it up to show him and a few other patrons who had turned to watch. Then she removed the paper from the bottom and popped the whole thing in her mouth.

She could barely closer her lips, but chewed quickly and the cake was soon gone.

"What sort of a trick is that?" he snorted, unimpressed.

She raised a finger to silence him. Then reached over and took a second cupcake. Again, she removed the base and ate the whole thing. This time, crumbs dropped down from the side of her mouth and onto the floor.

"Great," he said. "Now you're wasting my time and making a mess." The teenage girl had returned from the pantry and was looking on also.

"Nearly finished," Kat said, swallowing the rest of the second cake. She picked up a third cupcake. The girl looked like she was considering snatching it away, so Kat pushed it into her mouth, paper and all. Her cheeks bulged as she worked the cake out of its paper and down her throat. Then she reached in and extracted the paper base, dropping it in a wastebasket.

"Very entertaining," Stephen said, putting out his hand. "That will be £4.50 for the cupcakes."

"But you haven't seen the magic yet!" Kat exclaimed, wiping her mouth with a paper napkin. She walked back toward our table and beckoned for him to follow. "Now," she said with a flourish of her hand. "Look in Mei's handbag!"

Nine pounds was a lot to pay for a fairly lame magic show, but Kat was laughing so hard that she had to sit down. Stephen, placated when she passed him a ten-pound note, offered to throw in a round of coffees for free. Wiping tears from her eyes, Kat apologised to Mei, who insisted that Tshombe and I take a cupcake each as she nibbled on her own.

"So, Tshombe," I said after the drinks arrived. "You're really afraid of heights?"

He sipped his coffee. "It's not so much heights that I am afraid of, as falling from them. To be precise, it is the landing that I fear the most." Another sip of coffee. "Your head hitting the ground like a coconut and your brains spilling out."

"That seems a rational fear to me," Mei opined.

"My father says I am afraid of too many things. That is one reason he sent me here, to confront my fears."

"To be honest," Kat said, "your father sounds like a bit of a jerk."

I did not yet know Tshombe's background, but it was clear that his father was a person of some importance in Zambia.

"Many people have said similar things, worse things." Tshombe nodded. "Those people are in prison now." He paused for a second, looking each of us in the eye. "I am joking, of course. Actually, they are dead." Another beat, then his face broke into a broad grin. "No, no, I am messing with you."

I made a mental note to google his family when I had a chance. His father had sent him to confront his fears. So why were Kat and Mei here? Why was I? In my room, I had gone over the welcome materials but it was all about achieving potential and pushing at limits. Was learning psychology meant to help with that?

"I need to take a walk," said Kat abruptly. "Keep me company?"

The invitation was an open one, but Tshombe announced that he was trying out for one of the optional activities—a play or something—and Mei said she needed to make a phone call. We cleared our coffee cups and I followed Kat outside to the edge of the college grounds.

"You know those things will kill you," I said as a fluid movement brought flame to the old-fashioned silver lighter, her other hand cupping it against the wind.

"The cancer sticks?" Tendrils of smoke curled round her words. "Yeah, I know. Drink less, eat more vegetables. Exercise. Do all this and you'll live twice as long. Or maybe it will just *feel* twice as long."

I stifled a laugh, then took out my diary and jotted that down.

"What are you always writing in that journal?" she asked.

"Just notes, impressions," I replied. Back home,

Mrs Sellwood encouraged me to keep a diary. "There's something about the act of writing by hand," she told me, "transferring thoughts onto a page. It can help firm up a memory, organise your thoughts. Or it can liberate you from a bad experience." I recalled an image of Mrs Sellwood sitting opposite me, talking earnestly, as she always did. "If you can reduce something to words, put it outside you, then it can't hurt you." Naturally, I didn't tell Kat any of that.

"Will you let me read it?"

I hesitated. "It's not really written for anyone else. I hardly even read them myself."

"Them?" she said. "How many of these journals do you have?"

I was going to pretend not to know, but that would have been disingenuous. I numbered them all and though this book was the first of a new format, it was volume 87. "A few," was all I said.

"Is it all 'I did this, I did that,' or do you write fiction?" Another drag on the cigarette. "Any angst-ridden poetry?"

"I used to write fiction, but Mrs Sellwood said that in a diary it was better to be clear about what was real and what was not. As a kid, I loved stories about medieval England—King Arthur and the rest of it. I wrote one in which a young boy from New York is the only person who can pull Excalibur from its stone. He goes on to become a wise and beloved ruler. It was so much simpler than succeeding in real life. Stupid, I know."

We were silent, Kat looking into the middle distance once again, when she started. "What's that?"

I followed her gaze, across the courtyard to the clock tower, now lit by spotlights. "I don't see anything," I said.

"Up there, above the clock."

At the top of the tower, a narrow balcony looked out over the college. I squinted and then saw the flash of a yellow raincoat. It was too far to make out a face, but the shape and movement were unmistakable. "Is that Professor Cholmondeley?"

Kat finished her cigarette and stubbed it out. "Let's find out," she said, grabbing an umbrella from the rack at the college entrance and heading across the courtyard.

"Into the tower?" I called, but she was already halfway there.

I found my own brolly and followed her through the kind of light English rain that seems to come from every direction at once. By the time we reached the base of the tower, our clothes were damp. We stood next to a heavy wooden door that looked like it was made out of railroad ties. I had walked past it before, noting the contrast between weatherworn wood, rusted iron bolt, and the shiny new padlock that secured it. Right now, the lock was gone and the bolt was open.

A large sign on the door in black and yellow had an exclamation mark in the centre of a triangle and the words: "Danger—Keep out." It seemed unlikely that Kat hadn't seen this, but I cleared my throat to point it out.

Kat sighed. "If it's stable enough to take Cholmondeley's weight," she said, "then I think it's fine for us to poke our heads inside." Then her bottom lip began to tremble. "You wouldn't—you wouldn't make me go in alone, would you?"

The damsel-in-distress look lasted all of three seconds before she returned to addressing the door. A firm tug and it swung open with a squeak of protest from the hinges. She touched a finger to her lips, which were trembling no more, and stepped inside.

There are moments, looking back over your life, when it is like watching a horror movie in which a character is about to open a door and everyone in the cinema knows that something awful lurks behind it. He reaches for the doorknob. From his perspective, it's an entirely casual action—what could be more normal than opening a door? But the audience knows better. It's almost as bad as when a marginal character says, "I'll be right back"—though, in that case, you know the character is about to die.

I was at the threshold. The stone certainly looked strong. It had stood for hundreds of years—what were the chances that it would collapse when I happened to go inside? Better odds, I figured, than what Kat would think of me if I didn't. Holding my breath, I followed her into a dank chamber lit by a single electric bulb hanging from a nail driven into the limestone wall. An exposed wire ran from the bulb across the wall and up a set of stairs on the side farthest from the door.

We folded our umbrellas and crossed the room, empty except for some gardening equipment and a few tins of paint. As we approached the stairs, I looked up the tower and saw hollow, wooden steps fixed into the wall rising flight after flight, small landings at the right-angled turns, a dozen or so before they reached the top. More light bulbs dotted the way, complementing the dull outside light that entered through periodic gaps in the stone.

"What are we doing here?" I whispered to Kat.

She turned to reply when we heard footsteps. Professor Cholmondeley must be on her way down already, because they were far closer than they should have been.

"Quick," Kat hissed at me. "Under the stairs!"

At the time, I thought she was worried that the door would make too much noise and give us away. I took out my phone and was about to turn on the flashlight to look under the stairs when she put her hand over mine. "No phone," she mimed.

I nodded. The stairs must have supported the professor's weight going up; hopefully, they would not collapse as she came down. The position of the single lightbulb meant that the space beneath the stairway was in shadow, but frayed cobwebs hung from some of the stairs themselves. That's good, I told myself. Cobwebs are old spider's webs, long abandoned. No spider would want to make its home here now. Surely.

My skin crawled nonetheless. With a push from Kat and the sound of the professor's steps directly above us, I scurried under the stairs. Kat followed, her body pressing mine further into the shadows. We were crouched down in the darkness, her hand on my shoulder as she squatted behind me—for balance, or protection? Then I felt her finger running along the back of my neck, the hairs involuntarily standing up. I felt her breath behind me, close to my ear, while her other hand rested on the wall next to mine. Was she flirting with me? Even in the dark, I felt myself beginning to blush.

"Kat," I whispered. "Do you feel it too? There's some kind of connection between us. It's like I've known you for years rather than days." As I turned my head, her lips brushed my cheek and we—

Well, perhaps it's just as well I didn't say any of that. Because a nagging thought lingered as the words started to form. If one of her hands was on my shoulder and the other was on the wall, the thing running across the back of my neck was not her finger. I reached up with my free hand and pressed down hard, trying to avoid making a noise. I felt rather than heard a crunch, and whatever it was that had scuttled across me dropped to the floor. I bit my lip to prevent myself making a noise, just as the footsteps from above now came down the very blocks of wood beneath which we hid.

Two sets of footsteps. Following Professor Cholmondeley's sensible low-cut shoes, the hem of her yellow Mackintosh nearly touching the stairs—I caught myself wondering whether she bought clothes designed for smaller adults, or for larger children—came a second pair of boots.

"I must reiterate how important it is that you keep this to yourself," Professor Cholmondeley was saying. "I don't want any word getting out. All it will do is cause confusion. Given the scrutiny we are already under, that's the last thing I need."

"Certainly, Dr Cholmondeley," the man following her said. He had a deep voice and as he descended the steps, I saw he was wearing a hi-vis jacket and a safety helmet. "Though at some point you will have to inform the Council."

"You leave the Council to me," she said firmly. "I can handle them."

"I don't doubt it," he responded, reaching the base of the stairs and standing next to her. "When do you want us to start excavating?"

In the shadows, Kat and I held our breaths as they spoke just feet away from us.

"As soon as possible," Professor Cholmondeley replied. "Make sure you are quiet, and keep out of the way of our residents."

"Very good, Ma'am."

We heard the heavy door open once more, squeezing further under the stairs as more light came in from outside. Then with a flick, the man switched off the lights, exited with the professor, and closed the door, leaving us in pitch blackness. I exhaled, just as the outside bolt was drawn closed and the padlock snapped shut.

"Bugger," Kat said under her breath.

I woke up my phone to give us a bare minimum of light as we clambered out from under the stairs. "Remind me why I followed you in here?" I asked.

With a snap of her thumb, Kat's lighter now illuminated her face and the room in a flickering yellow glow. Her eyes watched the flame before regarding me. "There's something going on with this tower," she said. "What are they digging for? And why keep it secret?"

"More immediately, how do we get out of here?" I switched on my phone's flashlight but there was only one door. Looking around, I pointed it up the stairs. "Is it possible that the couple who died here got locked in also and were trying to climb down?"

Kat extinguished the lighter with a snap and pulled her own phone out now, dialling a number. "I doubt it," she said. "They could have called out for help, or phoned a friend—ah, here we go." She brought the phone up to her ear.

"Oliver, is that you?" She laughed into the phone and in the dim light I think she rolled her eyes at me. "Yes, well that favour I said I might need one day—I'm afraid I need it now."

Oliver, it transpired, was one of the porters who worked at Warneford. Kat explained that, through no fault of her own, she had come to be accidentally locked in the clock tower. No, no, she would explain later. Thank you *so* much. And a girlish laugh. Was she flirting with him also?

"He says he'll be here in fifteen minutes," she said to me. "Shall we take a look around?"

As I opened my mouth to reply, I saw that Kat was already halfway up the first flight of stairs. That seemed like a bad idea. I switched my phone's light on again and looked around for safety equipment, maybe a helmet like the one worn by the man just now, or at least a decent pair of boots. Then I heard Kat's heels turn the first corner and hastened to follow her.

The stairs, mercifully, were not medieval. An iron railing beside them also looked like a recent addition. The still air inside the tower was musty and cold. A rhythmic tapping noise accompanied our footsteps; when a drop of water hit me on the head I realised that the roof leaked. Beneath our feet the wooden stairs were damp. I looked up the central well between the stairs, shafts of light cutting across from narrow windows on the western side.

Kat was ahead, the light of her phone now bobbing opposite me in the stairwell. I had been testing each step before putting my weight on it, but now increased my pace to match hers and soon we reached the clock mechanism, pendulum dangling dolefully as its cogs rusted. Outside, I knew, its face still showed eight minutes past eight.

I half hoped Kat might stop there, but she carried on past the clock, emerging through a stone archway onto a narrow balcony that encircled the tower. I gasped at the view of Oxford, domes and spires stretching out before us. Even in the drizzle, there was a kind of melancholy beauty.

"It's something, isn't it?" Kat asked.

I turned off my phone's flashlight and snapped a picture. I had no idea when or if I'd get to see this view again. I was about to ask Kat if she wanted a photo of herself when I saw that she had gone to the edge of the balcony, where the wall alternated between higher and lower sections. I later read that these were called crenellations, allowing archers or other defenders to shoot while maintaining cover. Kat, however, was leaning out through one of the gaps, not to fire an arrow but to take a selfie with her head over the edge.

"Kat," I said, keeping my voice calm. "Any chance you could bring yourself back onto the ledge here? If they're worried about the tower collapsing, then perhaps leaning out over the courtyard isn't the best idea."

This time I could see her eyes rolling. She took her photo, droplets of rain gathering on her cheeks. "I love it up here, away from everyone." She took a deep breath, leaning further over the edge. "As a kid, I used to dream that I could fly. Stretch out my arms, take a leap, soar into the sky—far away from everyone and everything. Disappearing into the clouds. Did you ever have dreams like that?"

Of course I had. "I think everyone dreams of flying at some point," I replied, moving toward her with a hand outstretched. "That and turning up at school without any clothes on. But we don't normally test them out when we're awake."

"Do you mean flying or going to class naked?" Kat asked. When she saw I wasn't about to reply, she sighed. "Fine," she said, taking my hand to come and stand next to me away from the edge. "No flying today." She nodded over her shoulder toward a large black umbrella striding across the courtyard below us. "In any case, here comes our knight in shining armour. We'd best go down and play the grateful students."

We hastened down the stairs and had just retrieved our own umbrellas from the shadows in the storeroom when the heavy door opened. By his accent, Oliver was from somewhere in the north of England, greying in the temples but still in good shape.

Mom and Dad had told me that the porters at Oxford were often retired military officers and famously unflappable. I had written down in my diary one of Dad's favourite stories about the time Scandinavian royalty had come to visit Balliol College. A gentleman had arrived at the porter's lodge and asked to see the Master of the College, an old friend. "Please tell him that Carl Gustaf is here," the gentleman said. "Carl Gustaf who, if I may, sir?" the porter inquired, expecting a surname. The gentleman hesitated, then said, "Actually, it's King Carl Gustaf of Sweden." "Very good, sir," the porter replied, dialling the Master's residence, raising the receiver to his ear. "Hullo? Yes, I have a visitor for the Master here. It's King Carl Gustaf, Carl Gustaf..." He set the phone down and turned back to the gentleman. "Sorry, sir, what country was it you said you was king of?"

I smiled at the recollection of Dad's laughter, which had often rendered the punchline of the story unintelligible. Meanwhile, this porter, Oliver, was giving Kat a small lecture.

"One day, Miss Evershaw," he was saying, "you will learn that rules are to be obeyed. The door to the tower is to remain locked at all times."

"Why, Oliver," Kat declaimed. "Surely rules are to be *interpreted.* The problem was precisely that the door *was* locked. We clearly were unable to open it and so I don't see why you are being snippy with me. The problem is the Warneford rule that, if obeyed strictly, would have meant that Huckleberry and I would have starved to death in here."

He took her protestations in good humour. "Yes, well, if and when you decide to enrol in the Faculty of Law I'll be sure to put in a good word for you. In future, however, please stay out of the tower."

"We will," I said.

That seemed to satisfy Oliver, who poked his head outside and then ushered us back onto the courtyard. "I note for the record," he said to Kat, "that we are now even."

"Yes, Oliver," she replied, serious now. "And thank you again."

The porter took his leave, while Kat and I continued across the cobblestones. I looked around and wondered where Chester and the girl's bodies had fallen, but decided not to ask.

"Now," said Kat, turning to me, her umbrella swinging to the side. "Don't say I never take you to nice places."

"Yes," I nodded. "That was quite interesting."

"You do know," Kat said, "that when an English person says something was 'quite interesting', they mean it was completely rubbish?"

"Ah, no," I replied. "Then I meant I had—er, a cracking good time?"

That earned another eye roll. "Maybe stick to speaking American," she said. "Anyway, must dash—people to do, things to see. I mean, the other way around."

I raised a hand in farewell. I could have reached out to touch her shoulder, wipe a lingering raindrop from her cheek, but I did not. "See you later," was all I said.

I walked back the long way, past the front of college to where Kat had smoked her cigarette. The butt was still there where she had squashed it, a faint hue of her lipstick transferred from filter to pavement. In my bare fingers this time, I picked up the remnant and held it before me, the memory of her lips. I shook my head to clear the thought and dropped it in a bin.

Down the corridors once more, I returned to my room. As I opened the door, it brushed against a piece of paper that had been slipped under while I was out. A single sheet, folded in half. I opened it.

Like a ransom note from a previous century, words and phrases had been made out of letters cut from a newspaper and stuck on with glue.

BE CareFul

SHe ONly lies

I held the paper up to the light but there was no other writing, no signature. Someone had gone to some effort putting together this message. If it was a joke, it was an elaborate one.

I looked up and down the corridor but it was empty, the only sound my own footsteps, then the click as my door closed and the lock engaged.

3

"How do we know what we think we know?"

At the front of the small classroom, Professor Cholmondeley rose from her chair and waddled toward the window, her duck-like gait enhanced by the overcoat she wore against the cold seeping through Warneford's stone walls. It was now my fifth day at this camp and I still had no idea what I was doing here. Outside, fall had succumbed to winter; what remained of the afternoon sun was hidden by darkening clouds.

"This is, to some people, more a question of philosophy than psychology," she continued. "Bertrand Russell once set out to prove the foundations of mathematics and, after three hundred or so pages, got as far as establishing that one plus one equals two. Yet the question is also central to psychology: both in understanding mental processes that go on within our head as well as the disorders that manifest outside it."

The days were falling into a kind of pattern, even if

the activities themselves remained something of a blur. After breakfast, my calendar would beep and direct me to workshops, "sharing sessions", and such outdoor activities as were possible in the English climate. It was like a mix of Outward Bound and a TV confessional talk show—less fun than Jerry Springer. How this was meant to encourage interest in psychology I had no idea, but this afternoon's programme was billed as Professor Cholmondeley's introduction to the subject.

"Indeed," she was saying, "a fundamental question is whether those are two separate things; whether the mind is separate from the body. René Descartes thought so, and it was key to what he thought he could prove to be true." She paused expectantly, although she had not asked a question.

"*Cogito ergo sum*?" Mei offered.

The fairer of the two spiky-haired English boys snickered. About two dozen students were in the room. The rest were probably "sharing" somewhere else.

"I'm not sure what you find so amusing, Mr Farquhar," Professor Cholmondeley intoned. I checked later that this really was how his name was spelled. "'I think, therefore I am.' The fact that Descartes could think that sentence was proof of his own existence, or at least proof of the existence of his mind." She resumed walking around the classroom. "The problem is that, using such a method, it can be hard to prove anything else. That way, solipsism lies: the belief that one's own mind is the only thing that can be shown to exist—or, at its most extreme, that it is the only thing that *does* exist."

"What about the rest of the world?" Tshombe interjected.

"The people, the things we interact with daily." He slapped the desk with his hand. "The objects we touch."

"A solipsist would say they may or may not exist," she replied. "Or perhaps that they exist only in one's mind. Philosophers continue to argue about this, but most psychologists reject the extreme position also. Most accept that we have minds as well as bodies, though there is still lively debate over whether these are two separate things, and which is in charge. Does the mind control the body or the other way around?"

Sitting one row ahead of me and two spaces to the right, Kat was taking notes on a pad. Professor Cholmondeley had said that this session was optional for returning guests like Kat, but she insisted that she was happy to take part.

"Bah," Tshombe sniffed. "My body does not control me. I control my body."

"Are you so sure?" Professor Cholmondeley asked. "Many of our actions precede our conscious awareness of them. You certainly don't control your digestion or the circulation of your blood. You can control breathing, but only up to a point. Even for decisions we make—stand up, sit down, turn left, turn right—brain scans show that the signal to act has been sent before we are aware of it. It might be that the very notion of consciousness meaning control is the wrong way to think about our minds."

In the second row, Kat sneezed, apologising as she rubbed her nose.

Unperturbed, Professor Cholmondeley stopped walking and raised a pencil in the air as if it were a wand. "We like to think of our mind as if it is conducting an orchestra, playing a score that we have written." The pencil was now a baton, moving to an imaginary beat. "Apart from anything else, that would be a horribly inefficient way to exist. Think about the amount of information we would have to process just to make sense of the world around us. All of the sensory data coming from the world around us, all the information that our body sends up to our brain. It would overwhelm us. The first attempts at artificial intelligence used that approach, designing subroutine after subroutine to control every aspect of decision making in a computer. It was a complete failure."

Then I saw that Kat had used the noise of the sneeze to rip a page from her notepad. She folded the paper several times and wrote something on the outside.

Professor Cholmondeley resumed pacing the room. "The idea of a master conductor also ignores how we evolved and the way intelligence manifests in other animals. We may be smarter than dogs, and dogs are smarter than goldfish, but our brains still have a lot in common. Our human brains merely have an extra layer on top that we call consciousness.

"So, a competing theory of the mind is that it doesn't work top-down, like a conductor with an orchestra, but bottom-up. That our bodies have systems that work in harmony and filter information up to our brains, producing a consciousness that we can make sense of."

I saw Kat nudge the girl in the next seat and pass her the folded note. The girl—Dharshini, I think her name was—looked down at the paper and then up at me. Her head gave a little shake and, holding the note with two fingers as if she feared contamination, she handed it on to Farquhar.

Tshombe, at least, was still paying attention. “It’s more like jazz than classical?” he mused.

Professor Cholmondeley laughed. “Maybe so. Different musicians improvising without a conductor. That is essentially how neural networks approach artificial intelligence today.”

Farquhar took off his glasses to regard the paper, holding it up as if examining it for invisible ink. To his right, Kat coughed loudly. But it was me that he looked at, turning with a grin. What was that German word Kat had mentioned? Farquhar opened the note and scanned the contents, the corners of his mouth rising still further. Then he blew me a kiss and crumpled the paper into a ball.

Backpfeifengesicht—a face in need of a good slapping.

“For our purposes,” the professor was saying as she passed Farquhar’s desk, picked up the crumpled paper, and dropped it in the rubbish bin by the window, “the mind-body debate affects how we see disorders. In particular, a problem may act on the body or the mind. If you ingest certain drugs, then your perceptions will change; if a person’s brain is damaged, then he or she might have difficulty walking or speaking. Yet our minds are also affected by non-physical traumas: some forms of verbal abuse can make us mentally dysfunctional. And so on.

“Consider how we think of treatments. Some disorders we treat through counselling—reaching out through words to the mind. Some, we treat through pharmacology—using chemicals to address an imbalance in the brain.”

"And some," Kat interjected, looking directly now at Farquhar, "we hook the patient up to an electrical socket and zap!" Her body shook as she mimed being electrocuted.

"Ah yes, Miss Evershaw," Professor Cholmondeley moved to stand next to her. "I had forgotten that you were taking sarcasm as a second language. Your studies go well, I see?"

"I've started learning German," Kat replied meekly, her theatrical performance concluded.

"And to think this time last year you were mastering Latin. *Sehr gut. Dr Freud wäre hocherfreut,*" the professor said. (I looked this up later and it was some kind of joke about Sigmund Freud being pleased.) "You do raise an important point, however indirectly. Electroconvulsive therapy got an unjustly bad reputation because of its depiction as a tool of abuse in *One Flew Over the Cuckoo's Nest.* Today, it is generally regarded as an effective treatment for certain forms of depression—but we are still not entirely sure why it works."

She resumed her movement around the classroom and landed by the bin near the window, looking out at the fading light. Rain had begun to fall. "In addition, your point about German—irrelevant as it may have been to our discussion—does raise an additional complication posed by the English language when it comes to knowledge. When we say, 'I know' something, it is terribly imprecise. Philosophers sometimes draw a distinction between 'knowing that' and 'knowing how'. It's the difference between having read a book about bicycles, knowing that they are propelled by pushing one pedal then the other while balancing on the seat—and actually knowing how to ride a bicycle.

"But since we are talking about consciousness, about identity, it is another kind of knowledge entirely to say that we know *someone.* To say that you know a person is quite different from just knowing certain facts about them. I may know that George Clooney was born in 1961 and first appeared on television playing a doctor, but it would be very odd indeed for me to say that I 'know' Mr Clooney if I have never met him.

"When we say we know a person, we usually mean we have some kind of relationship with them. That may be why, when that person passes away, we switch tense. After a person dies, we don't say we 'know' them; we say we 'knew' them."

"A little like love," Kat said softly. "You love someone while they're alive. But when they're gone, you say you loved them."

"Very good, Miss Evershaw." Professor Cholmondeley was standing close to Kat and now rested a hand on her shoulder, a strangely familiar gesture. Then the hand lifted and the words continued. "And to your point about German, it uses different words for that kind of knowledge—*kennen* rather than *wissen.* Now, how does this connect with our ideas of consciousness?"

The room fell silent and I pulled my own attention away from the bin with Kat's note in it. "What if," I began, feeling the words out as they left my mouth. "What if consciousness isn't some kind of free-form jazz going on in our heads. That might be what happens in animals, but there must be something more than that. It's more than harmony and improvisation. What if consciousness is like—like a story that we tell ourselves, a way to make sense of the world and our place in it?"

"Interesting," Professor Cholmondeley said. "What would this mean for our relationships with other people?"

"Knowing someone," I said, "relationships, love. They're the stories that we tell each other."

"A plausible hypothesis worth exploring," she said as a chime from her phone indicated the end of the seminar. Kat later told me the chime was a recording of the now-silent Warneford clock tower. "Perhaps one that we will discuss on a future occasion."

The other students began to head for the door, but Professor Cholmondeley indicated for me to wait. I had my eyes on the bin anyway, and took my time putting things into my backpack. Kat, Mei, and Tshombe were lingering also—Tshombe obviously waiting for me, Kat and Mei absorbed in their phones.

"I gather you are something of an English history buff," the professor said as she moved to switch off the light.

"I suppose," I replied, though it wasn't framed as a question.

She nodded. "Then you might be interested that there will be an exhibition next week at the Ashmolean Museum on the Magna Carta. It's one of the oldest documents we have—there are four copies from 1215 still in existence and I gather that one of them is coming to Oxford. That's pretty old, even by Oxford's standards." She cast her eyes around the room once more and flicked the switch. "It's also a useful reminder of how writing can help make things last. When we commit words to paper we fix them in time, we bind them in a way that memories are not bound. Eight centuries later, people are still reading those words. Remarkable." She nodded and took her leave, waddling off down the corridor.

As she turned a corner, I ducked back into the seminar room and looked in the rubbish bin. Next to a browning apple core sat the crumpled note. I picked it up and flattened the paper. "Huckleberry" was written in an exaggerated copperplate on one side. Unfolding it, I held it up to the fading light, not hearing Kat enter the room also until she stood beside me. "This was a private message," was all the note said. "You'll pay for reading it without permission."

"What were you expecting?" Kat inquired. "A little poem? Something angst-ridden? 'Roses are red, violets are blue; sugar is sweet, and so are you?' Ugh."

"So why write a note if you knew it was going to be intercepted?" I asked.

"Ah Huckleberry," Kat sighed. "You can be very boring, you know that? I wrote the note *because* I knew it was going to be intercepted. Now I get to plot my revenge. What do you think it should be? One of the classics: itching powder in his bed, or ordering fifty pizzas in his name? Or something more modern, like subscribing him to a few dating websites with a photograph of the young George Clooney?"

"I think you have way too much time on your hands," I said. What I didn't say was that a small part of me had wanted the note to be for me. I put it in my pocket anyway.

"They brought a copy to Singapore once," Mei said as the four of us began the walk back to the dormitories. "I read that it travelled strapped into a first-class seat with a security guard and was displayed behind bulletproof glass. I asked my parents about going to see it, but they said I had to study."

It took me a moment to realise what she was talking about. "You mean the Magna Carta? How long was it in Singapore?"

"A week," she replied.

"You had to study the entire time?" Tshombe's eyebrows seemed to rise of their own accord, independently of the muscles on his face.

Mei looked at him blankly. "Well, with school, tuition, taekwondo, orchestra, and service projects, it does make a trip to the Supreme Court a bit tricky." His eyebrows showed no sign of descending, but she shook her head. "They were right to push me. I needed to be pushed."

"And that's why you're here now," Kat observed, a wry grin creeping across her lips.

"Partly," Mei conceded. "The only reason I did well at school was because they pushed me." Her eyes closed, debating whether to share what came next. "I remember," she continued, "coming home from primary school with my first test paper. I was so pleased to have gotten 93 out of 100 points." She grinned, revealing perfect white teeth. "The teacher had drawn a smiley face next to my name." The teeth disappeared behind lips now pursed. "I showed it to my father, who nodded and then asked me to get the cane from where it hung on the wall." Her hands flexed at the memory of it. "One for each mark I had lost."

Tshombe nodded. "So, your father and my father were not so different. Though you knew when it was coming. My father beat me, but not for test papers. He beat me for disappointing him. I find it very hard to predict what will cause such a reaction—to be honest, I'm not sure he even knows himself." Now he shook his head, before turning to me. "What about you, American. I was told that Americans do not hit their children now—and that is why you are all so spoiled. Is that true?"

The idea of either Mom or Dad resorting to violence was absurd—their glasses would have fallen off. Yet it didn't seem like a time for laughter. We reached a junction in the corridor near the bedrooms, where the guys would turn one way and the girls another. "No," I said, "they didn't hit me." I looked down at my hand, fingering an old scar. "They would *reason* with me. Appeal to my better self. It started with incentives—endless charts of my behaviour with rewards like chocolate and punishments like no screen time. Stickers here, stickers there. Then it became financial, pocket money and fines. And lectures on how teenagers suffer from impulse control difficulties because the prefrontal cortex is still developing."

The scar was long healed, but the memory of pain when I had punched the wall remained. "Sometimes I wished they would just shut up and hit me. It might have been easier. For all of us."

"At least you all had parents," Kat said softly. "My first memory is of the fire. Clutching my teddy bear as the house burned down, flames consuming my childhood.

The sound of my own voice calling, 'Mummy? Daddy?'..." her words trailed away as she looked up at us, tears welling in her eyes. Then she snorted with laughter. "Nah, I'm making that up. Jeez, compared to all of you my parents were completely boring. My Dad basically regards life as an interruption to sleep."

What was the German word Mei used for someone who told inappropriate jokes that they themselves found endlessly entertaining? I flicked back in my journal to where I had written it down: *Witzelsucht.* Like her, however, I decided to avoid confronting Kat with this opinion.

In any case, she had moved on. "So," she was saying, "are you going to see this Magna Carta thing? I gather you Americans are crazy about it—rule of law, hold the King to account, and all that."

"Maybe," I said. To be honest, all I could remember about the Magna Carta from high school was that Oliver Cromwell had dismissed it a few hundred years later as the "Magna Farta". England's legends had always been more interesting to me than its actual history.

From outside, the first rumble of thunder echoed through the building, a low timpani dampened by the stone walls. The lights flickered, reminding me of the tower and its spare illumination.

"What was that?" Tshombe's eyes darted to the ceiling.

"Old wiring," Kat said reassuringly. "Buildings like this weren't designed for electricity. When they did put it in they sometimes laid the wires behind new stonework. The result is that it's very hard to maintain and occasionally the power just—"

There was a flash of light outside the window and a crack that sounded more like a snare drum. Then the lights went out.

"—fails," Kat completed her sentence as the corridor disappeared into darkness.

I felt a sharp pain in my forearm. Tshombe had grasped it so tightly that he was cutting off circulation.

"Is everything OK?" I asked, breaking the silence that had followed the lightning strike. With my free arm, I took out my phone and switched on the flashlight. Tshombe's whitened knuckles released me and he put his hands back in his pockets, continuing to shift uneasily on his feet.

I was going to ignore the incident, but Mei also had her phone out and was looking at him curiously. "Are you afraid of the dark also?" she asked.

Tshombe sniffed. "No, I am not afraid of the dark," he said, as if offended by the thought. "I fear what hides in the dark. The serial killer, lurking in the shadows, biding his time, sharpening his razor, waiting to leap out and slit my jugular."

Mei's eyebrows lifted. "That's a fairly specific fear," she said. "But if you were trying to kill someone—especially if it was your hobby—you would be more likely to aim for the carotid artery than the jugular." She saw the expression on our faces and added, "I read a lot of true crime novels growing up."

I was about to reply when the lights flickered back on. "See? Circuit breaker," said Kat with a degree of confidence I doubt she felt.

We had been at the point of splitting up, but I was a little wary of being alone with Tshombe in case the power went out again. I suggested heading to the common room, a kind of lounge with easy chairs and newspapers. Warneford's bedrooms were somewhat grim spaces, probably designed to encourage us to spend more time in the shared areas of the college. The other three assented and we climbed the stairs together.

The common room had large windows looking out over the courtyard. During the day, this maximised the light; in the twilight, as it was now, the windows framed the courtyard and the clock tower rising above it, lit from below by spotlights that emphasised the irregularity of its stonework. This evening, however, the lights were out. Peering out at the rain, which was now coming down strongly, I noticed a half-dozen men carrying equipment into the room at the base of the clock tower from a small truck parked nearby.

One piece looked like an oversized drill of some sort, but I couldn't make out the rest. A generator? They lugged their gear inside, shut the door, and then a thin band of light burst through the bottom of the doorframe, broken occasionally by shadows moving within.

Tshombe, bored with the storm, was entertaining himself by looking through the cupboards below a small pantry area when he froze suddenly. "Oh my goodness," he exclaimed.

I turned, half expecting him to be cowering from a spider. But my own eyes widened when I saw what he had found. "They have a Nespresso machine here?" I asked, incredulous. "Then why on earth have we been drinking that dishwater at the café?"

Mei had sat down in one of the armchairs and was flipping through a tabloid newspaper. "Machine yes, pods no," she said without looking up. "Or rather, the pods are under lock and key for 'special occasions'. I guess they don't want a bunch of students amped up on caffeine running around in the middle of the night."

Kat moved beside Tshombe and took a butter knife from the sink. A row of drawers sat above the cupboards, four of which were locked. "Eeny, meeny, miny, moe..." she said, before slipping the blade into the gap at the top of the fourth drawer. In a matter of seconds it was open and she held up an aluminium pod.

"How would sir like his coffee?" Kat asked me with a bow. Then she straightened. "Alas, since there's no milk or sugar, I'm afraid it will be black and in a paper cup."

"Just like George Clooney," I said with a grin.

"George Clooney drinks coffee from a paper cup?" Mei put down the newspaper. "Oh, you were being sarcastic." She nodded thoughtfully. "Very droll." I think that was intended as a compliment, but I'm still not sure.

"So, Huck," Tshombe asked. "Do you believe what you said about consciousness?"

I savoured the smell of it, the texture of the crema. "What, about consciousness being a story we tell ourselves?" I took a sip. "I don't know. I was kind of making it up as I went along. Do you actually believe that there's a jazz band playing in your head?"

"You're both talking rubbish," Kat said as the machine burbled away in preparation of her own coffee.

"Consciousness is nothing. We think consciousness is important because common sense tells us that it is. But common sense also told us that the Earth was flat and that the sun revolved around it. Consciousness is evolution's way of stopping our heads exploding—the illusion of control. The worst thing is that we're complicit in this, we lap it up. Consciousness is a confidence trick—and we're both the grifter and the mark."

Her coffee made, the machine fell silent and the room with it.

"I'm not sure you can be both a grifter and a mark," Mei said at last, folding her newspaper. "Your confidence trick metaphor requires two conscious beings to make sense, which I assume was not the point…" She trailed off. "Oh, were you being sarcastic again?"

Kat had taken her coffee to the window and was looking out at the clock tower.

"What about you, Miss Mei," Tshombe said to break the silence. "What do you think of consciousness?"

"Me?" Mei replied, putting the newspaper back on the shelf. "I think us trying to understand consciousness is like a goldfish looking out of its bowl and trying to understand how the television works. Lots of time for speculation, but no way of proving anything. And we'll forget all about it in a couple of minutes, anyway."

Tshombe looked at her. "Hmm. I think I prefer my jazz idea to all of yours. Goldfish indeed."

It was almost time for dinner, served in the hall where we had first met. The artifice of seating us together on that first day was a blatant attempt to nudge us toward friendship, and yet it worked. Where was this friendship heading? If consciousness really was a story we told ourselves, and our relationships were stories we told each other, what sort of tale would this be?

And Kat. Kat of the raven hair and pale English skin and not-quite-perfect teeth. Kat, whose humour was self-deprecating until you saw you were the one being deprecated. When we hid in the tower together, her hand resting on my shoulder, I had hoped that there was something between us. In my mind I played out propositions, declarations, buttons of her blouse popping open of their own accord. I sometimes caught her staring at me, yet when I did, she had a way of making me feel as though I had been the one staring at her.

Tshombe, whose fears appeared to include the possibility that he might go hungry, broke me from this reverie by pointing out that dinner was about to be served downstairs. He had a rehearsal scheduled, right after dinner, and did not want to be late. So we headed down to collect our plates and join the queue.

Afterward, Kat announced that she was going for a fag—a cigarette—but didn't ask for company. As I watched her walk away, I felt a pain in my chest.

Tshombe had elbowed me in the ribs. "You should ask her out," he said. "Take her dancing or to see a show. Something classy."

Mei was at his side. "Alternatively, you could follow the English tradition," she added. "That would mean both of you getting so drunk that you can plausibly claim not to remember anything and then make your move."

I looked at my two new friends, both earnestly attempting to help me out. Evidently I'd been hopeless at hiding my interest in Kat. Still, I was content with denial.

"You're both wacko," is all I said.

If they were offended they didn't show it. "Oh yes," Tshombe admonished me. "The story you are telling yourself at present is that you and Kat are just friends. But the way that your eyes trail after her shows that this story is at best a half-truth. Once again, my jazz metaphor explains it best. Your eyes are playing 'Can't get enough of your love, babe'."

"Wack"—I repeated—"o." But as I returned to my room the ache where Tshombe had elbowed me was replaced by a lightness. I lay on my bed and recalled Kat's face, a finger drawing a stray lock of hair from her cheek. Yet this time the finger was my own.

Later that evening, after showering and reading, as my eyes grew heavy, I wondered about sleep. What happens to consciousness when we allow it to ebb away in the night, surrendering to our dreams. Does the conductor drop his baton for the night? Is it the end of a set in Tshombe's jazz concert? Or maybe it's just the end of a chapter.

4

It wasn't the scream that woke me, but the silence after the scream. I sat up in bed, the room lit only by a sliver of light peeking through curtains that I now drew wide. My room looked onto the street, a nearby lamppost flickering in the driving rain.

In flannel pyjamas and bare feet, I padded down the corridor toward the girls' rooms. My eyes soon adjusted to the dim green light of emergency exit signs, my footfalls the only sound. My phone still sat by my bed, asleep and recharging. As I rounded the corner, a row of doors stretched ahead of me with nameplates I struggled to read in the darkness.

How had I heard Kat from such a distance and known with certainty that it was her? How was it that no one else had woken? These questions I put aside as I slowed to check each door until I found "Catherine Evershaw". I raised my hand to knock but it swung open at the first touch. A blast of cold, damp air struck me in the face as I entered; the windows were opened wide to the storm, swirling papers and clothing around the room. The bed was slept in, but empty. I touched the pillow where her head had rested, now wet from the rain.

Pulling up the collar of my pyjama top, I looked out the window. The ground floor room opened directly onto the courtyard. In a flash of lightning I saw a figure moving across it, the rumble of thunder echoing as darkness returned. I clambered over the windowsill to follow, bare feet cold on the stone.

"Kat!" I called, but the wind was against me. Flannel quickly becoming soaked, I ran across the courtyard, gaining on the figure, but not before it reached the base of the clock tower and entered the open door. By the time I passed the warning at the threshold, she was halfway up the stairs.

Uneven wood cut into my feet, pyjamas clinging to my skin. My leg ached. Still I climbed, sucking cold air into my lungs until I reached the last flight and burst out onto the rain-lashed balcony. In another flash of lightning I saw her standing on the ledge, looking out over the skyline as the wind played with her hair. She turned a damp cheek and beckoned me to join her, outstretched hand reaching for mine.

"What are you doing?" I shouted above the maelstrom.

She simply smiled and reached her hand out further. "Take my hand," she said. Somehow, I heard her over the rain and the wind.

I took a step closer, shivering as adrenaline was displaced by the cold. "Kat," I said more calmly. "Please come down from there."

"Take my hand," she repeated, turning once more to look out over the courtyard and beyond.

"Why don't we go back inside and we can hold hands," I said.

I was closer now, and could see tears mixing with raindrops on her cheeks.

"Take my hand and come with me."

"Come where?" I asked, but as she looked over the precipice I knew what she meant.

"It's the only way we can be together, forever," her voice was too soft to be audible and yet I heard her clearly. That should have told me that something was not quite right, but it was also when I felt the warmth of her hand in mine.

Together, we stood on the ledge as the wind buffeted us. "Kat," I began, but a finger on my lips silenced me.

"Shhh," she whispered in a voice that was surprisingly deep. "Everything's going to be OK. I think that your bedtime story to yourself this evening was some kind of nightmare, but you will be OK. Maybe you should have stuck with jazz like I suggested."

She was only inches from me now, yet her face was becoming indistinct, a picture going out of focus. I still felt my hand in hers, but the tower, the rain, and the wind all began to blur and fade until the only thing left was her hand. I grasped it more tightly, but now it changed also, becoming larger so that my own hand felt small within her grasp, a strangely comforting sensation. Until I felt the roughness of her skin also and realised that it could not be—

"Tshombe?" I sat up in bed, releasing his hand.

The door to my room was open and Tshombe, wrapped

in a terry towelling dressing gown, stood by the side of my bed. "Trust me," he said. "I am far more relieved than you. For a moment it looked like you were going to try to kiss me."

"What happened?" I asked, turning on the bedside light. "Did the storm freak you out also?"

"What? No, I do not get 'freaked out' by a bit of water and static electricity," he replied. Even in the shadows, I could see the air quotes he mimed. "You were shouting," he continued, sitting down in the chair by my desk. "Like you were having a fight—or trying to stop one. I knocked on your door but there was no answer."

"How did you get in?" He wore a black wristband like me, but they were meant to open only one's own room.

He shrugged. "I used one of my father's credit cards to open the door. They are not very secure." He held up a Visa card, an edge of which was now dented.

"I'm sorry I disturbed you," I said. "It was just a dream."

"That much I guessed," he said. "Is it something you want to talk about?"

I hesitated. "Not particularly."

He nodded and stood up to go. "Some people think," he said, standing at the doorway, "that dreams reveal our deepest desires, things we might not dare to do while awake. Others that they help us work through our fears. And then there are some people who believe that dreams are only the noise produced as our brains store memories away, like defragmenting a hard drive. Which sort of dream was yours?"

Now it was my turn to shrug. "I'm not sure," I said, honestly. "Maybe a bit of all three."

Again, Tshombe nodded. His willingness not to pry was, I knew, not a lack of interest but a kind of respect. "Good night," was all he said.

"Good night, Tshombe," I echoed. "And thanks."

As he closed the door behind him, I reached for my journal. The memory of a dream can be like holding water in your hands, so I quickly noted down some of what I recalled. By the time I had finished, I was too awake to sleep.

I checked my phone by the bedside, its battery indicator glowing a contented green. It was well after midnight in Oxford, but early evening in New York. I decided to phone Mrs Sellwood. For whatever reason, she had not replied to my emails. But her phone number was in my contacts list and we had not spoken since I came to England. I was sure she wouldn't mind.

As the phone rang, I tried to imagine where she might be. I knew very little of her personal routine. She was married, I thought, but I didn't know her home address or if she had any children of her own. It wasn't exactly my business, of course.

"Hello?" It was a man's voice. Her husband, perhaps? Or a boyfriend?

"Ah yes," I said. "It's Huck—Huckleberry Jones calling. Can I please speak to Mrs Sellwood?" If it was her boyfriend, this could be awkward. There was the noise of traffic in the background; it sounded like the man was outside.

"Mrs Who?"

"Mrs Sellwood," I repeated. "Please tell her Huck is calling from Oxford."

"Listen kid." The voice now sounded irritated. "I don't know how you got this number or who you think you're calling, but there's no one here by that name and you'd better not call again."

The line went dead.

I had her office number also, but it was long past work hours. Maybe she had decided to retire her cellphone after all, I thought. She often spoke of how our addiction to phones and social media gave the illusion of connection with the world, when in fact it left us feeling more isolated. At school, I certainly knew people who spent more time cultivating their Instagram feeds than getting to know flesh-and-blood friends.

I put the phone down and considered trying to sleep. That seemed unlikely, so I put on a pair of shoes and a coat over my pyjamas to take a walk.

I don't think it counts as déjà vu if you know your previous experience was a dream, but it was still uncanny walking down the corridor as the rain continued to pour outside. It was the differences as much as the similarities—the green of the emergency exit lights, shadows cast by the window frames.

Resisting the temptation to go past the girls' rooms and try Kat's door, I headed toward the front entrance. Light came from under the door of one of the offices. I heard a voice, recognising it at the same time Professor Cholmondeley's name became legible on the plaque.

"Everything is proceeding according to plan," she was saying. "We should be finished before Christmas." It was a phone call, though whose number she might have dialled at this hour was unclear. "Yes, I am acutely aware of how important this is. We can't have another incident like last year." Another pause. "No, that is now resolved. Chester's parents accepted the settlement and agreed not to sue." A brief pause then, with some irritation, "Yes we included an NDA."

So, the parents of the boy who fell from the tower had agreed not to bring a lawsuit or talk about it in exchange for a payment. What about the girl?

"The new batch?" The professor's irritation was brief, as she continued more thoughtfully. "They're settling in as well as can be expected. Some adjustment difficulties are inevitable, but I think most are becoming acclimated to their new home. I think they'll manage just fine."

Another pause. "The wristbands? Working well as far as I can tell. No one has complained, if that is what you mean. Hang on, there's someone outside. Can we finish this another time?"

I contemplated fleeing but the door opened and Professor Cholmondeley's head poked out. "Huck?" she said. For an older woman, she moved surprisingly quickly.

There was no point hiding, so I replied, "Good evening, Professor."

"You should really be sleeping," she said. "But from the look of you that is proving difficult. Would you care for a hot chocolate? I just made myself one—a little reward for completing some reports."

That is how I came to be sitting, past midnight, in Professor Cholmondeley's office, sipping hot chocolate from a mug. The office was sparsely decorated, the only idiosyncrasy a small cactus sitting on her desk.

"Is anything troubling you?" she asked, sitting back in her own chair and taking a sip from her own mug.

The dream, my feelings for Kat, why I couldn't reach Mrs Sellwood. "No," I replied. "Everything's fine. The storm was keeping me awake."

She took another long sip. Much of psychology, I was discovering, involved listening; listening in turn meant getting people to talk. I raised the mug to my lips also, trying to appear comfortable in the silence. For the first time, I could look closely at the ring she wore on her index finger. Silver and aged, it had a simple cross that was a faded red. She turned it absently as we sat and listened to the rain outside.

"The earliest humans were astonished by the weather," the professor said at last. "They feared it. They worshipped it. Lightning cast down from the sky they explained as Zeus, angry at the world, hurling bolts forged for him by the Cyclops. Closer to home, massive edifices like Stonehenge were built to celebrate the sun—and pray that it would continue to return, day after day."

I now knew Professor Cholmondeley enough to see that she was not recounting this information to pass the time. She was going somewhere.

"Today we have scientific theories to explain the weather," she was saying, "and we are somewhat better at predicting it—though we've made virtually no headway in controlling it. On the contrary, with global warming we seem hell-bent on making things worse. One good thing about a dramatic storm is that it can put our troubles into perspective. Seeing that we are small creatures in a big world can, perversely, be comforting for some people."

"Really, I'm fine," I said, meeting her gaze.

Now it was she who looked down, suddenly interested in aligning the folders on her desk. "Have you been keeping in touch with your parents?" she asked.

"Of course," I lied.

I should phone them, I thought. I owed them that much. "They're staying in town for a few days before heading back to New York. Mom also gave me a new journal. I think it's her way of trying to maintain a connection. You know, part of a routine, so that the last thing I do at night is think of her." I realised how that might sound and corrected myself. "Not in, like, an Oedipal way or anything. Just that I hadn't forgotten her."

The professor laughed. "Sometimes, Huck," she said, "a cigar is just a cigar."

"Freud, right?" I asked.

"Yes. It's not clear that he ever said anything of the kind, but it's a useful reminder not to read too much into ordinary events, or to take ourselves too seriously." She finished her drink and stifled a yawn. "It's very late," she said. "I suggest you try to ignore the storm and get some sleep."

I drained my own mug. "Thanks for the hot chocolate." I stood to go, but stopped when I saw the print hanging next to her door. It was an architectural drawing of a tower.

"Is that the Warneford clock tower?" I asked, hoping that my level of interest sounded casual.

"It is," she replied. "As you probably know, the tower far predates Warneford itself. It was originally part of a church constructed in the early thirteenth century. This is a reconstruction of the original design."

The diagram was a cross section, showing the tower rising at one end of a circular main building. "And that was the church?" I asked.

"Yes," she said. "The round design was typical of Templar churches of the time."

"The Knights Templar?" I had read a little about the order, which enjoyed the reputation of great secrecy while also being linked in popular culture to everything from the video game Assassin's Creed to the location of the Holy Grail.

"Now, now," the professor stood up and waddled over. "Don't get too excited. Dan Brown caused us a lot of trouble with his *Da Vinci Code* nonsense. We still get the occasional nutter coming around looking for the direct descendants of Jesus. The Templars were the bankers of their day, so they had money. And in those days, if you had money you built churches."

I looked at the plan again. "So, the round building got torn down at some point, but the tower remains." I traced the outline with my finger from the crenellated battlements down to the ground. And then below. "There's a structure below the tower?" I asked, trying for innocence.

Professor Cholmondeley now stood next to me and gestured toward the door. "Perhaps," she said. "But this is a copy of an early attempt to reconstruct the original design. We don't know what's down there. Probably nothing.

Unfortunately, the whole structure is unsound. That's why it's strictly off limits for students."

On the diagram the underground chamber appeared several times larger than the room at the tower's base. I leaned forward and could make out the word "crypt".

"As I said," she added, "it's late and you should get some sleep."

I stepped out into the corridor. "Thanks for the drink."

"Good night, Huck." She switched off the light in her office, locked the door, and headed toward the exit with a large umbrella tucked under her arm.

I considered asking if she needed assistance, but the professor was better prepared for the weather than I was. Instead, I retraced my steps to my room, holding up the wristband until the door clicked open. To help my eyes adjust to the dark I did not turn on the lights, but as I entered, my foot slid on a piece of folded paper. I picked it up and examined it in the light of my phone. Once again, it was a short message composed with cut-out letters. Once again, it was a warning, though who had sent it or why was another mystery.

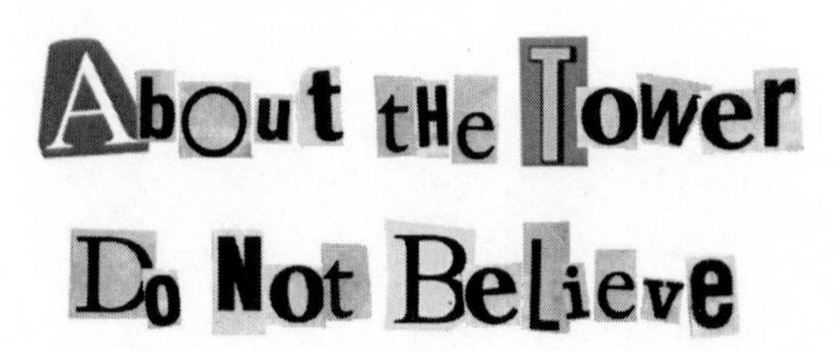

Believe what? I quickly opened my door and looked down the corridor, but if anyone had been there I would have seen them earlier. Was this Tshombe's idea of a joke? I resolved to ask him the next day, refolding the note and putting it in the desk drawer with the earlier message.

Outside, the lightning had stopped, but the rain continued as a low drumming on the roof. I took off my shoes, hung up my coat, and lay down on the bed, waiting to see when sleep would come.

5

"'Magna Carta is the most famous legal text in history'," Tshombe said, reading from a brochure that he had picked up at the porter's lodge. "'Signed eight centuries ago by King John at Runnymede, near Windsor'—that's between here and London, right?—'it laid the foundations for constraints on arbitrary power: the basis for the rule of law, democracy, and human rights. From medieval to modern times, it has been invoked by those struggling against injustice around the world, from Mahatma Gandhi to Nelson Mandela.'"

It was the morning after the blackout and we were at breakfast. As had become usual, Tshombe and I sat with Kat and Mei. By unspoken agreement neither of us mentioned the previous night. It was entirely possible that he had picked up the brochure to be certain we would have something else to discuss.

"This Magna Carta sounds quite interesting," he continued. "My father should probably read it sometime.

Do you think that they will let me take a photograph with it?"

"Of course," Kat enthused. "You should totally take a selfie with it—hashtag 'LatinLover'."

Tshombe ignored her and kept reading the brochure to himself.

"That was sarcasm again, right?" Mei checked. "I think I'm getting the hang of it now. In any case, Tshombe, I doubt that they will let you take a photo with the real Magna Carta. Maybe they'll have a facsimile you can use. In your photo, no one would be able to tell the difference I bet."

Tshombe set aside the brochure. "But then it would not be authentic," he said.

"Speaking of authenticity," Mei said with the eagerness of a student piping up in class, "there are a few problems with that brochure you were reading. It's not quite right. By which I mean, well, all of it is wrong. When they brought that copy to Singapore, I did an assignment. Did you know that the Magna Carta wasn't intended to limit power at all, but preserved the king's rule? And though many paintings show him holding the Magna Carta and a quill, King John never signed it. Oh, and it wasn't called Magna Carta, either."

"Look who isn't Little Miss Wikipedia!" Kat seemed impressed.

"I do not understand," Tshombe said. "You did an assignment on this Magna Carta for homework, but your parents still would not let you see the real thing?"

"Water under the bridge." Mei waved her hand. "I got an A-star on the paper and my parents bought ice cream that night. So, it all turned out fine."

"How old were you when this happened?" I asked, remembering my own parents' efforts to limit ice cream consumption when I was young.

"It was last year," Mei replied.

There was silence as we digested this. "Wow," I said. "Your parents really are tiger mom material, weren't they?"

"Ma and Ba aren't so bad." She shook her head. "They want what's best for me."

"It could be worse." Kat took a sip of coffee. "My father left us when he ran off with a girl two years ahead of me at school." Her eyes began to moisten.

"I thought you said your parents died in a fire?" Tshombe asked.

"No," Mei said. "She said her parents were boring and that her father regards life as an interruption to sleep."

"OK, maybe I'm exaggerating," Kat conceded. "But I'm pretty sure he lusted after her in his heart. Anyway," she said to Mei, "you ended up here, right? And like they say: Oxford is what turns you from a stereotype into an archetype."

"Who says that?" Tshombe asked. "I have never heard people say anything of the sort."

"Well, *I* say it, then."

When she thought no one was looking, Mei wiped her own eyes with a shirtsleeve. "What else were you going to say about the Magna Carta?" I asked.

She sniffed and took a sip of her tea. "Just that the main reason the Magna Carta became so famous was because no one bothers to read it—especially the Americans who came to love it the most."

"Oh, that's hardly surprising," I said. "We're very good at not reading things."

"No, I'm serious," she continued. "The American revolutionaries like Benjamin Franklin fell in love with the document, or at least what they thought it represented. And so a hastily negotiated peace agreement between a King and the barons threatening him became the foundation of American liberty."

"Well," said Kat, "as the only English person here that benefits directly from the Magna Carta, which is still part of the law of the land—"

"Actually," interrupted Mei, "the rights were mainly for the barons, who were aristocrats and tended to be French. Also, it wasn't particularly good on women: it says something to the effect that you can't rely on a woman as a witness for any crime except the death of her husband—"

"As I was saying," Kat cut in, "given that I am the only English person here, you might be interested to know another reason the Magna Carta remains a subject of fascination. And that is why it worked. Why King John was allowed to remain in power. He was one of the weakest kings in English history—you know what they called him in public? 'Softsword'. So why didn't the barons just kill him?"

Tshombe tugged at his lower lip. "It sounds like he was in a bad negotiating position. He was facing a rebellion and had to agree to limit his power in order to keep any of it. The barons got what they wanted and he got to stay on the throne. That sounds perfectly natural to me."

"Yes, but most of what he gave up was so trivial," Kat said.

"We studied this at school also. And the original Magna Carta reads like a shopping list. Some of the demands were individual complaints by the barons, but it goes on and on about having a common measure for wine and beer, the width of cloth, how to catch fish in the Thames, and stuff like that."

"Maybe that's how the barons approached it," Mei said, though she sounded less confident. "They weren't looking to impose grand reforms but to protect their interests."

"Exactly." Kat brought her hands together. "So, how is it that a few years later this mishmash of an agreement starts being called *Magna* Carta—the 'Great' Charter. Something else was going on at the time, some other piece of a larger puzzle."

At that moment, Professor Cholmondeley glided up to our table. "Jigsaws for breakfast, Miss Evershaw?" she inquired. Then she noticed the pamphlet Tshombe was holding. "Ah, I see you have discovered an interest in our historic document. Are you considering a visit? We can make provision for that, I suppose."

"Yes," Tshombe said. "Particularly if I can take a photograph with it to send to my father."

A frown crossed the professor's brow. "It's an eight-hundred-year-old parchment," she began, "I suspect they will be quite cautious to ensure that it lasts a little bit longer than its visit to Oxford."

"This is one of the only four originals left from 1215, isn't it?" Mei, ever the diligent student, inquired.

"I believe so," Professor Cholmondeley replied. "In addition to this one, which is travelling from Salisbury

Cathedral, there is one at Lincoln Cathedral and two in the British Library."

"But they are all identical?" Mei pressed.

"More or less," the professor said. "As I recall, there were once a dozen or so originals. This was before printing, of course; scribes would copy text down and then the royal seal would be attached. So the different versions were written by different hands; the words are essentially the same. I gather Salisbury's is one of the best preserved. A copy in the British Library was badly damaged in a fire a few hundred years ago. Why someone would put such a priceless item anywhere near a fire is beyond me, but there you go."

She looked at her watch and turned to leave. "Now, apologies, but I have a class to get to." As an afterthought, she called out to me. "Oh, Huck?"

I stood and hastened over to her side, unsure whether I should stoop down to bring our faces to the same level. I ended up doing so, if only to hear her more clearly, for she spoke in a lower voice than usual. "I see you managed to get some sleep in the end?" she began. It was not a question. "Huck," she hesitated, searching for the right words, "I think your mother did a fine thing encouraging you to write a journal. Putting words on a page is a good discipline for the mind; some say it can also be balm for the soul."

I wondered if this brief conversation had been the reason she came by our table in the first place. I nodded an acknowledgement and returned to find that Mei and Tshombe had finished their breakfasts and left. Kat raised her black coffee to me in a wordless toast. I raised my own mug and we clinked porcelain.

"You know," she mused, "I'm glad we ended up at Warneford together."

The room suddenly felt a little hot.

"Oh," I said, trying not to blush. "Why do you say that?"

"You're one of the few people who will breathe my passive smoke," she laughed. "But also, I feel like I've known you longer than a week. It's strange. Strange in a good way, I mean. But strange nonetheless."

"I think I know what you mean," I said. "I feel comfortable around you also."

"Anyway, somehow or other you ended up here, so maybe that's lucky for me."

As she said this she reached over to take the container of sugar from next to my coffee, brushing my fingers as she did. "You don't take sugar," I said.

"I'm unpredictable," she replied, tipping some into her mug and stirring it with a teaspoon. She removed the spoon and brought it to her lips, sucking it clean like a lollipop. And, with her green eyes on mine, she took a long drink—and spat the coffee back into the cup. "Oh my god. How do you drink that sugary muck?"

Now I laughed. It was a while since I'd flirted with anyone. Even as a distant warning alarm sounded in my mind, I enjoyed the moment and her gaze. Sometimes, the things that hurt us most are precisely the ones that give us the most joy.

The feeling of warmth carried on through the morning, a blur of classes and activities. The rhythm of a day at

Warneford was now established—sharing sessions, activities, meals—but its purpose remained obscure. At times it felt like we were there to learn; at others, it was like we were the ones under the microscope. Our parents had obviously paid good money for us to spend almost a month at Oxford, what return were they expecting on this investment?

Early that afternoon I got a text from Mom that she and Dad were coming to visit before they flew back to New York, so I resolved to ask them.

And then there were the notes. I separately asked Tshombe, Mei, and Kat about receiving messages under their door and drew blank stares. If it was a practical joke, it was a bizarre one. I wondered if one of the spiky-haired English boys might be behind it, though cutting up letters from a newspaper seemed like a lot of work.

By the time my parents reached Warneford it was early evening. They came in a taxi from the train station after a trip to Stratford-upon-Avon and a Shakespeare matinee.

"Why didn't you rent a car?" I asked, helping Mom down. "You guys used to go on about cruising around the Cotswolds, or wherever that photo of you in the convertible was taken."

Dad shrugged. "I offered to drive. But your mother prefers the famous English public transportation system." He added in an exaggerated stage whisper: "That's why we're late."

"I think we've got enough to worry about without you trying to drive on the wrong side of the road," Mom replied tersely, giving me a kiss on the cheek. "Now, how have you settled in?"

"Fine, fine," I said as we walked up to the common room. We passed Dharshini, humming to herself in the hallway, who nodded a hello. "To be honest, I'm still not quite sure what you think I'm meant to get out of a month here."

"Think of it as a camp," said Mom.

"A very expensive camp," Dad muttered.

"A break from school, from life at home," Mom continued. "A chance to explore yourself in a different way."

I digested this. "Well, I'm not sure about exploring myself, but I guess I'm learning a bit about psychology."

"That's kind of the point," Dad said.

Why were they now so keen for me to study psychology? Back in New York, Felix and the guys who weren't off skiing or bumming around were doing programming. Maybe when all the jobs were taken by computers, enough people would be driven crazy to keep the psychologists in business.

I considered telling them about the notes under my door, but it would only freak them out. They were heading back to New York soon.

"So what are the other kids like?" Mom was saying.

"Nice enough," I said, even as Farquhar walked into the common room and stuck his tongue out at me. Juvenile. "It's a pretty random assortment."

I also considered telling them about Kat, but that would have been a whole other can of worms. A couple of years earlier, Dad had tried explaining sex to me, obviously having been instructed to do so by Mom. After acting dumb and asking how birds and bees could reproduce without getting stung, I assured him that there was plenty of material I could consult on the internet about human relationships. He agreed to let it go at that, but suggested that we go for a walk anyway so that Mom didn't yell at him. So we walked down to the Hudson, watched birds fighting over food scraps, then walked back home. It was one of our better chats.

"We fly to New York tomorrow, but you can text or call us any time. And we'll be back here in time for Christmas." Mom was still talking, upbeat as ever. "There's a dinner and figgy pudding. One year when your Dad and I were here it even snowed. Remember that, Robert?" She touched his sleeve, but he was a million miles away. Turning back to me, she added, "Promise me that you'll use the journal, write things down like we talked about?"

I nodded.

"Will you promise me that you'll write down something about seeing us today? Us coming to say goodbye until Christmas?"

"Sure," I said. And I did.

6

Oxford University's Ashmolean Museum was the first public museum in Britain. More than three centuries ago it was established when Elias Ashmole offered the university his cabinet of curiosities, complete with a stuffed dodo. At the time he received an uncertain thank you, but dictionaries of the period were soon using the collection to define "museum", a word still new to the English language. This much I read as we lined up—queued up—for tickets, after passing through blue doors beneath an imposing portico supported by columns that were meant to look Greek.

It was a week after my parents' visit. Classes and activities continued, late-night activity in the tower continued, and another person had been stabbed outside a pub, but otherwise it was an uneventful seven days. The stabbings worried some of the students and there was talk of exercising greater caution, but compared with mass shootings in the US it was all pretty tame. No lockdown measures, no active shooter drills—just stay away from anyone who might be carrying a knife.

Kat remained a mystery. What I had thought was her flirting with me had gone further only in my imagination; I was beginning to wonder whether the flirting itself had been imagined also. She was friendly, laughed at my jokes, and we walked together when she smoked. But afterward she always had to rush off somewhere. A couple of times, I caught her looking over my shoulder when I wrote in my diary. She said she wanted to know if I was writing about her, then pretended not to care if I was.

As the start of the Magna Carta exhibition approached, Tshombe insisted that we be there for the opening. "It's an eight-hundred-year-old piece of paper," Kat sighed. "You can't wait a few more days for the crowds to die down?" But Mei was also keen and got Professor Cholmondeley's permission to miss classes. So it was that we found ourselves at ten o'clock on a freezing Tuesday morning in a queue that stretched out the door and onto the street.

"I still don't understand why you wouldn't let me get the tickets online," Mei muttered, stamping her feet against the chill.

"As I have explained to you," Tshombe replied, "everything you do on the internet is tracked to make a gigantic file about your life. This is used by the Americans to spy on you—no offence, Huck—and by the Nigerians to steal from you."

Kat also stamped her feet, but out of irritation. "The line is taking forever." She took a newspaper from her shoulder bag and turned to the comics.

I looked ahead to where the snaking column of students, tourists, and pensioners reached the ticket counter for special exhibitions. A harried woman with a forced smile was processing tickets while also answering questions. Beside her, two staff members were idly checking their phones. I explained the delay, wondering aloud if it might help to suggest a more efficient use of labour.

"That's interesting," Mei said, "because I've been working on a theory about the difference between the English and Americans."

"Oh yes?" Kat said. "Pray tell."

Mei looked at her warily, then pressed on. "The English like to moan. That is, they enjoy grumbling about things—but grumbling with no expectation that anything will change. The weather is a typical example, but so is the bureaucracy at Oxford, or this queue. Americans, on the other hand, Americans are different."

"How so?" I asked.

"Americans don't moan—they complain," she said. "When Americans are upset about something, they complain until something changes. That's why they're always suing each other in court—a lawsuit is the ultimate complaint."

It was a pretty big generalisation, but there was some truth to the caricature—the English were certainly polite, though they also included some of the most miserable people I had ever met. "What about Singaporeans?" I asked. "Where do they fit in this theory of yours?"

"Oh, that's easy," she replied. "Singaporeans don't moan or complain. Whenever there's a problem, we make a suggestion and then await instructions from the government. The response is either to announce that they've got a plan to fix the problem, or that we were mistaken in thinking there was a problem in the first place."

"Well?" Kat said looking at me. "How about you go be an American and complain about this queue?"

"In a minute," I said. "First, I want to hear where Zambians fit in this theory."

Mei frowned. "I don't know enough about Zambia itself, and I've only got a sample size of one." She nodded at Tshombe, who was absorbed in his phone.

Then he looked up. "There," he said. "Now come with me." He left the line and started walking toward the entrance.

"What about the tickets?" Mei asked.

"Zambians know that there is no point moaning or complaining, and definitely not making suggestions. We get off our backsides and do something about the problem ourselves. So, I have just purchased our tickets online and we may proceed to enter."

"But what about the Americans and the Nigerians spying on you and stealing your credit card and your identity?" she said.

"I used my father's credit card," Tshombe said. "The Americans are surely spying on him already and the Nigerians are welcome to try to steal his money."

With that, he led us into the museum and upstairs to where a florid "M" marked the beginning of introductory text about the Magna Carta. Eight hundred years old, foundation of the rule of law, parts of it still in force in England, and so on. Mei snorted at an illustration of King John, quill in hand, about to sign the document as benevolent barons looked on.

A bored guard stood at the entrance, checking tickets. Kat sidled up to him, unnecessarily swishing her dark hair as she did. "So, officer," she pouted, "don't you want to search me?" He raised an eyebrow, then self-consciously looked up at a dark hemisphere protruding from the ceiling. "Oh," Kat nodded. "Big Brother is watching, eh? Do tell me, are you the only one guarding this old piece of paper? That must be a big responsibility."

Tshombe showed the mobile ticket purchase on his phone, which the guard dutifully scanned.

The guard nodded at the ceiling. "Me, Big Brother, and a bulletproof glass cabinet bolted to a concrete wall," he said. "I think we'll be fine."

"I feel *so* much safer," Kat said, blowing him a kiss as we entered the next room. Was she trying to get a rise out of me, or just playing a trick on the guard? In hindsight, it should have been clearer what she was planning. But you don't generally assume that a friend is about to rob a bank just because she waves to the police standing outside.

Inside the exhibition proper, large panels described the history of the Magna Carta before and after 1215—the subsequent versions over the years, its rediscovery in seventeenth-century England, the journey it made across the Atlantic to appear in Benjamin Franklin's *Almanac.* On a table under spotlights, someone had built an elaborate recreation of the site in Runnymede where the negotiations had taken place. We turned a corner and there were yet more panels about medieval England, the rule of law, and the emergence of the English language.

"We have paid good money to see a lot of posters," Tshombe grumbled. "And that papier mâché construction looked like a child's unfinished railway set."

"It's possible that they felt the need to beef up the exhibition," Mei said, "because the Magna Carta itself is quite—"

"It's so small!" Tshombe exclaimed as we turned another corner and saw the document itself, at the end of a room framed by an elaborate screen with yet more text. The parchment was the size of a newspaper, about sixteen inches by twenty. As we approached, we could see the cramped text that filled most of its surface, except for an inch of space running along the bottom.

"Small parchment, big impact!" enthused a museum guide who stood near the glass case. "Or were you perchance expecting a tapestry?"

"I was expecting a little more than this," Tshombe confessed, leaning in to examine the document more closely. "It looks like someone tried to cram as many words as possible into a tiny space. Was paper very expensive back then?"

"It is not paper," the guide said with a laugh. "It is vellum—calfskin. Did you know that even today our laws are written on the same kind of parchment? Acts of parliament governing air travel and the internet, still inscribed in the same way that King John agreed to limit his power more than eight centuries ago."

“Why did the barons get him to sign it?” Kat inquired.

“Ah yes, well that is one of the great misconceptions about Magna Carta,” the guide, whose badge bore the name Ganesh, replied. “You see no one actually signed it. Unfortunately, the museum commissioned that picture you walked past before they asked me to help with the exhibition. What King John did was affix his seal to show the authenticity of the—”

“OK, so why did they get him to affix his seal?” Kat asked impatiently.

“He didn’t have much choice, did he?” Mei interjected. “The barons had already taken most of London and popular opinion had turned against John. In order to keep the throne, he had to give in to some of their demands.”

“That is correct.” Ganesh, the guide, nodded. “The barons were in a far stronger position. We now believe that the barons drafted several versions of a document limiting the King’s powers that eventually became Magna Carta. One of these drafts turned up in France for the first time only a century ago.”

“That’s not what I mean,” Kat said. “Why did they let him stay in power—why didn’t they exile him or kill him?”

“Oh,” Ganesh paused. “Well, the barons themselves were only barely united. It is likely that they regarded a weak King as preferable to a power vacuum. So, when the King agreed to let Archbishop Langton mediate—”

“Langdon?” I interrupted. “As in Robert Langdon?”

Ganesh looked at me, and then laughed. “You mean the dude from the *Da Vinci Code*? Harvard professor of 'symbology'? No, it was a real person and his name was Lang*ton*."

Once again, Kat rolled her eyes. "Is it true," she continued, "that the night before the negotiations, King John slept at the headquarters of the Knights Templar?"

"Why, yes it is," Ganesh replied, with a look of pleasant surprise. "I tell you, it really is nice to meet people genuinely interested in the history of the document. So many of our visitors just want to take a selfie and then move on."

Tshombe coughed. "Now that you mention it," he said delicately, taking out his phone.

"I am afraid not," Ganesh said, raising a hand. "You are welcome to buy a replica in the gift shop and you can do whatever you want with that, but we do not allow photos in here."

Mei raised an eyebrow but resisted the temptation to say, "I told you so."

"Back to the Templars," Kat said with a note of exasperation. "One of them accompanied King John to the negotiations also, didn't he?"

"Not only accompanied, he helped write the document." Ganesh's enthusiasm returned as he pointed to the parchment behind its glass. "If you look at the opening text, you'll see his name. Here we are: '*Johannes Dei gracia*'—that's 'John, by the grace of God,' blah, blah, blah, for the health of our soul and the better ordering of our kingdom, and so on. Then there is a list of his advisors. Here we are: '*fratris Aymerici magistri milicie Templi in Anglia*'—that's 'Brother Aymeric, master of the knighthood of the Temple in England'."

"What is so special about these Templars?" Tshombe had put away his phone and was reading one of the panels next to the glass.

"Basically, they feature in every conspiracy theory about global history," I said. "They stole the Holy Grail, they run the world's banks, they are the Illuminati—very big with the tinfoil hat crowd."

Other visitors were now approaching the display case, but Ganesh seemed interested in talking a little more. "The Order of the Poor Fellow Soldiers of Christ and of the Temple of Solomon, better known as the Knights Templar," he began, "were a group of soldiers who fought in the Crusades—a series of wars fought during medieval times in the hope of reclaiming the Holy Land from Muslim rule. Individual knights took a vow of poverty, but the Order itself controlled vast sums of money—effectively becoming one of the first banks. When Magna Carta was negotiated, they had been around for a hundred years and controlled most of King John's assets. A hundred years later, however, they had grown too powerful and France's King Philip—who owed them a lot of money—contrived to wipe them out."

"How?" Tshombe asked. "If they were so powerful, why did they not fight back?"

"King Philip launched a surprise attack," Ganesh said. "Something like arrests in organised crime cases today, most of the leadership were arrested or killed on the same morning: Friday the 13th of October 1307."

"Friday the thirteenth?" Tshombe repeated. "Unlucky for them."

"Many people believe that is the origin of the superstition," Mei said.

"I thought that came from the Last Supper," I said. "You know, Jesus dining with thirteen people just before Good Friday?"

"Most likely it's a modern invention," Ganesh concluded. "It has been nice chatting with you, but I had best speak to some more of our guests."

We nodded our thanks. "Can I ask one more question?" Kat asked, her face now an inch from the bulletproof glass. "What do you know about the theory that there was more at stake in these negotiations than fishing rights and standard measures. That King John gave up far more than this in order to stay on the throne."

Ganesh shook his head. "I do not know what you mean," he said. "King John agreed to the demands that were put before him."

"But what if there were other demands not recorded here, or recorded secretly," Kat pressed. "What if King John gave up something even more precious than being above the law?"

"A secret agreement?" Ganesh frowned. "I think that is highly unlikely. Scholars have been working on Magna Carta for centuries—I think we would know if there were any such agreement. Anyway," he said, flashing a mouthful of white teeth, "nice talking with you." He turned to the next group of visitors—Australian tourists, by the accent—"So, small parchment, big impact, eh?"

Kat, Mei, Tshombe, and I continued through the rest of the exhibit, which described the impact of the Magna

Carta around the world and its influence on popular culture. Quotes from Gandhi and Mandela stood somewhat incongruously alongside Jay Z's "Magna Carter" tour poster.

Afterward, Tshombe was keen to find a copy with which he could take a photograph, but Mei suggested we head to the gift shop via the Chinese Paintings Gallery. Kat said she needed to use the bathroom and would catch up with us.

For ten minutes or so, Mei led Tshombe and me around the gallery, which seemed to consist entirely of pictures of mountains with streams running down them, streams running beside them, or streams running under them. Mei tried to explain the subtle differences, but I could see that Tshombe, like me, was struggling to feign interest.

We had reached an entire wall covered in blue and white pottery that reminded me of some Dutch crockery my parents owned when an alarm went off. The high-pitched whine lasted several seconds, after which the eerily calm voice of an Englishwoman was broadcast through the museum: "Ladies and gentlemen we request your attention. A fire alarm has been activated. Please proceed to the nearest exit and leave the building immediately. Kindly refrain from using the elevators at this time."

Even in an emergency, the English were polite. As the message repeated, Mei and I crossed the gallery and were almost at the emergency exit door when I realised that Tshombe had not moved.

"Tshombe!" I called, but he did not respond, his eyes still on the pottery.

I ran back to his side, Mei not far behind me. "Tshombe," I said more calmly. "Time to go."

A bead of sweat was trickling down his temple as the message played a third time.

"It's probably a false alarm," Mei added, trying to be reassuring. "But in case it is a fire, we should leave now. Old buildings like this often burn surprisingly quickly, or collapse in on themselves, killing everyone inside."

"Maybe let me do the reassuring talk bit," I said to her, putting a hand on Tshombe's shoulder. "Tshombe, we're going to be fine, but we do need to go. It's fine if you're afraid of fire, but let's talk about it outside."

His whole body was tense. "Not fire, smoke," he whispered.

"Yes, well where there's smoke there's fire," I said. "But, again, let's chat about this outside."

"It is the smoke that kills you," Tshombe went on. "More often than fire, it is the carbon monoxide in the smoke kills you. Not such a bad way to go, I am told. Far better than being barbecued alive."

"You make a good point," I said, taking one of his arms and pulling it over my shoulder to turn him toward the exit. "Now, shall we?" But his size-thirteen feet remained planted on the stone floor.

"I have an idea," Mei said. "I saw it work once with someone who was frozen in panic." She moved to stand in front of Tshombe. "Tshombe," she said firmly, her right hand angled backward, "snap out of it!" And she brought her hand up to slap him hard across the face with a crack that could be heard even over the alarm.

Tshombe shook his head, eyes at last focusing on Mei and then on me. "Thanks," he said simply.

Together, we ran to the exit. The bar on the door warned an alarm would sound if it was pressed, but that seemed irrelevant now. Tshombe opened the door to a set of concrete stairs that soon deposited us outside on a back lane. We followed the lane around to the area outside the main entrance where people were gathering. There was no sign of smoke from the building and the crowd seemed remarkably orderly. There was no sign of Kat, either.

As the stream of people leaving the museum began to diminish, I saw Ganesh, the museum guide, walking briskly down the steps. He recognised us and turned in our direction.

"This is all a bit more exciting than we'd intended for the opening!" he said, white teeth flashing again. I wondered if it was a sign of nerves.

"Don't you need to stay with the Magna Carta?" Tshombe asked. "Protect it with your life and so on?"

"Good gracious no." Ganesh laughed at the prospect. "I'm a doctoral student working here part time. They don't pay me enough to do anything like that. In any case, the cabinet in which it is displayed is bulletproof, fireproof, and bombproof." He turned to me. "You are American, right? We modelled the storage on your Declaration of Independence, though as usual the US goes several steps further. Every night your Declaration is lowered into a fifty-ton steel and concrete vault that can withstand a nuclear bomb. It is a wonderfully American idea that the world might be destroyed, but at least the Bill of Rights would survive."

"Have you seen Kat?" I asked. "Black hair, fair skin, lots of questions?"

Ganesh shook his head. "Sorry, I haven't. She had some interesting ideas. If she's keen on pursuing them I think there are some likeminded folks to be found in the madder corners of the internet." His phone beeped and he looked down at it. "Apologies," he said. "I am expected to assemble with the museum staff. Your friend will surely turn up."

As Ganesh left, I tried calling Kat but her phone was off. This was not in itself unusual—she would occasionally turn off her phone when she did not want to be disturbed. In the circumstances, however, it did little to ease our anxiety.

Wailing sirens heralded the arrival of a fire truck and two police cars. Four firefighters with helmets and flame retardant jackets jogged into the museum while the police moved to stand near the entrance. The security guard from outside the exhibition walked down to greet them, looking nervous.

"Ladies and gentlemen." It took a moment to identify where the announcement came from, until I saw a middle-aged man with a bullhorn. "We apologise for the inconvenience. There has been a small fire in the museum, now contained. We regret that we will be closing for the rest of the day. For those of you who purchased tickets for our special exhibitions, unused tickets can be returned tomorrow for a full refund. Thank you for your attention."

He lowered the bullhorn and, with a collective sigh, many of those assembled began to shuffle off. I weaved between them to catch him before he went back into the museum.

"Sir," I called out.

He paused at the blue doors. "Can I help you?" he asked.

"A friend and I got separated during the evacuation, I can't find her."

"Oh dear," he replied. "Does she have a phone?"

"It's off."

He hesitated. "I can tell you that no one appears to have been injured. We are still completing a sweep of the building, but the fire itself was quite localised. Are you and your friend visiting Oxford?"

I explained that we were staying at Warneford.

"Oh, I see," he said slowly. "Well in that case, I'll let them know. In the meantime, I suggest you return to Warneford and see if she shows up. The building has half-a-dozen emergency exits to different points outside. It is possible that she is there already." With a nod, he turned and went back into the museum.

Tshombe and Mei caught up with me. "What did he say?" Mei asked.

"To head to Warneford in case she turns up."

We walked down the stone steps toward the street. This took us past the police, who were now talking urgently with the security guard. As we passed, the only snippet of conversation that I heard was one of the officers asking him why someone would deliberately start a fire in a lavatory. I turned my head to see his answer, but he said nothing, mouth opening as the colour drained from his face. We were out of earshot, but I saw him leading the police into the building at a sprint.

Putting two and two together may be simple math, but

hindsight is always easier than foresight. At the time, I think I was worried about Kat, frustrated at the lackadaisical evacuation plan of the museum, and uncertain what to do next. The English have a nice expression about a penny dropping—a reference, I gather, to old slot machines in which a stuck penny is at last accepted by the machine, connecting a phone call or dispensing a toy. Well, mine remained firmly stuck.

In any event, I suggested that Mei and Tshombe take the bus back to Warneford while I stayed near the Museum. I tried her phone a few times but it remained off. Then, as I was about to head back to the college myself, I got a text:

Meet in your room – 15 minutes. Tell no one. K

I called her phone again but continued to get a message that it could not be reached. I hailed a cab and was soon back at college and returned to my room. I felt bad not telling Mei and Tshombe that I at least knew Kat was OK, but her message had been clear. Why she should be so mysterious, I still had no idea. Again, in hindsight, I feel like an idiot, but I'm trying to be as truthful as I can.

As the minutes ticked by, I sat down at my desk. Opening my laptop, I searched for "Magna Carta" and "Templars", with Google offering up tens of thousands of search results. Some of them looked a bit dubious, but there was clearly some serious research in the area. One website essentially claimed that the Templars were responsible for the modern rule of law, noting that half of England's barristers and judges were members of Inner Temple and Middle

Temple—institutions on land once owned by the Templars and created in the years after the Templar order itself was disbanded. I was about to click through yet another link when there was an urgent knock on my door.

I opened it and Kat burst in, her face red with exertion and excitement. She was breathing heavily. "I've got it," was all she said.

"Got what?" I asked, the penny still stuck in the slot.

She dropped her shoulder bag on my desk and took out the newspaper she had been reading earlier. English newspapers are usually folded like American ones, but this had now been rolled into a cylinder. Still not comprehending, I watched as she put the cylinder on my bed and flattened it out. Then she delicately turned to the centre pages. On the left was a story about the latest royal baby, a source of endless fascination in England. The right-hand page was something about a fight with the European Union—another favourite topic—but it was obscured by a yellowed sheet of thick paper that sat atop it.

"It's not paper," I heard myself say. "It's vellum—calfskin." Eyes involuntarily widening, I looked at Kat, who simply nodded. "My God, Kat. What have you done?"

She put her hands on my arms, our faces only inches apart. It was the first time we had touched since hiding under the stairs in the tower and brushing fingers over breakfast. I felt my own face start to flush as the smell of her hair enveloped me. Thoughts of stolen property, police breaking down the door, years spent in an English jail were driven from my mind. Then she let go of me and fumbled for something else in her bag.

"The Magna Carta," I said dumbly, leaning down to look at it more closely. Without the glass it was possible to see the individual strokes of ink crowding the page. I closed my mouth to avoid breathing on it. "How did you—Why did you—?"

I turned and saw what she had taken from her bag. It was a strange time to have a cigarette, but she was holding her lighter.

"Now," she said evenly. "You hold the edges while I set it on fire."

Part Two

Now

"How did you think this was going to end, Huck?"

My eyes are shut, but the harshness in the voice still makes me wince. Below us, the carollers on the street outside Warneford's walls have started up again. "Away in a Manger", it sounds like. One of my favourites.

Tentatively, I open my eyes. Soft rain has collected on my cheeks, indistinguishable from tears. In my hand, the wet parchment feels fragile.

"I didn't kill him." The words barely leave my mouth. That doesn't make them less true.

"I beg your pardon?"

"I said I didn't kill him," I repeat, more confidently. Though that doesn't make the words any less pointless.

"Of course you didn't, Huck." The voice is soothing now, calming, yet with the slightest hint of mockery. "You were in the wrong place at the wrong time, weren't you? Holding a knife, covered in his blood."

"It wasn't real," I say. My confidence is waning. "None of it was real."

"Of course. It was all a story. Play-acting. Imagination."

"Yes," I nod, turning around. For a moment, hope raises its deceitful head. Just for a moment.

"But there are still consequences, Huck." The voice hardens again. "For every action, there is an equal and opposite reaction. For every wrong, there is a remedy. And for every disease, there is a cure."

Was I wrong? The carollers are reaching the end of their song. Bless all the dear children and fit us for Heaven. I'm a bit beyond that now, I suppose.

It's funny how memory can play tricks on you. Two people can share the same experience and yet remember it completely differently. Can that happen to one person? Can you remember something in two different ways?

"You were given ample warning, Huck," the voice continued, the boots stepping toward me. "You can hardly say that you were treated unfairly."

For every disease, there is a cure. And then I see what I need to do. I see how this ends. A tragedy, to be sure, but a forgivable one. Huck must have slipped. He climbed the clock tower at night. Perhaps he had been drinking. It was foolish, but no one's fault. No shame in his memory; no disgrace for his grieving parents.

My hand gripping the wet stone, I climb onto the ledge. I am directly above the clock face: eight minutes past eight, as it always has been, and as it always will be.

"That's right, Huck." The voice is a serpent in my ear. "It will all be over soon. You do know how this ends after all."

Once more, I look down at the courtyard, its cobblestones waiting to embrace me.

Then

7

Many years ago, I did an assignment on Robert Frost's poem, "The Road Not Taken". It's his most famous work, a favourite of middle school English teachers. Students are particularly fond of the final lines:

Two roads diverged in a wood, and I—
I took the one less travelled by,
And that has made all the difference.

It appeals to teenagers because it seems to celebrate individuality, freedom, choice.

It seems to, but it does not. Because the poem isn't really about any of those things—it's about regret. The hint is in the title: the poet's focus is on the road *not* taken. Opportunities missed, experiences forsworn. Ages and ages hence, an old man looks back and wonders, with a sigh, whether he should have gone the other way.

As I look back now, how many roads did I miss? On how

many chances did I pass? If I now had the ability to time travel, is there anything I could have said to my earlier self that might have helped?

But there is no such time machine, and the future is what it will be. So, instead of chasing Kat and her stolen property out of my room, or calling the police to arrest her, I asked why she proposed to set fire to an eight-hundred-year-old parchment.

"You want to do what?"

"Set it on fire," Kat repeated. She was breathing heavily, but her eyes gleamed.

"You stole this and now you want to destroy it? It's probably worth millions of dollars—I bet I'm going to prison even for standing here with you. And you want to incinerate it?"

"No," she said, more calmly. "I want to find out its secret."

I looked at the parchment more closely. It certainly looked like the Magna Carta I had seen through bulletproof glass earlier in the day. "How did you steal it, anyway? Is this real?"

"I took that dopey security guard's key," she replied.

I recalled her flirting with him, but to take a key from a security guard without him noticing couldn't be easy.

"They had to have a backup plan in case it was necessary to evacuate quickly," she continued. "So, after I set off the fire alarm, I waited to make sure he was gone, unlocked the cabinet, and here we are."

"They gave that guy a key to the cabinet?" I asked.

"I know," she nodded. "Pretty lax security. That's what

made me decide to do it. They were practically asking for it to be stolen."

"And the cameras?"

She laughed. "They'll get some lovely footage of a borrowed coat lifted up over my head. I removed the parchment, wrapped it up nice and safe in the newspaper, and here we are."

It was incredible. No, it was insane. But the vellum on my bed even smelled like calfskin. Not that, admittedly, I knew what eight-hundred-year-old calfskin smelled like.

"OK," I began, hesitating for a second, wondering in the back of my mind at what point I became an accomplice. "What do you think this secret is?"

"The 1215 Magna Carta never made any sense," Kat said. "King John was weak, the barons could have had anything they wanted. And yet they settled for so little. Later versions of the Magna Carta had real provisions on the rule of law, jury trial, and so on. The first version had none of that. Even smarty-pants Ganesh couldn't explain why King John was allowed to remain in power."

"So, what's your point?"

"To get the barons to agree, there must have been something more. Something important. Today we think that the Magna Carta is the foundation of the rule of law. Back then, the King was above the law. He was accountable only to God."

I had dim memories of something called the divine right of kings. The monarch today was still the head of the church, but no longer thought of as divine. "I thought that was the point of the Magna Carta, establishing that everyone—even the King—was subject to the law."

"Yes," she said. "But you can't just say that God is subject to the law. Before the King could be bound, you needed to sever that relationship with God."

My head was starting to hurt. "And that's what you think setting fire to the parchment will reveal?"

"No, but I think we will see what King John agreed to in 1215." She brought her lighter down toward the parchment and prepared to ignite it.

"But why fire?" I protested, reaching out to hold her wrist back.

"Brother Aymeric," she said. "The one Ganesh was talking about. He was the senior Templar in England at the time, but virtually nothing else is known about him. The name is very unusual, but has a German origin. In particular, it is very similar to the Old High German word *Eimuria.* That means a funeral pyre. A relative in English is the modern word 'ember'."

"OK, so the guy's name might mean fire. But what makes you think that's a secret instruction to set the document alight?"

"Because there's no other reason for his name to be there. The other people listed in the document all had religious or royal titles: bishops and archbishops, earls and lords. Why is a mere brother listed also?"

I looked down at the text. My Latin was non-existent, but I could see where the rise and fall of the quill spelled out Aymeric's name at the end of a series of other dignitaries. "I thought the Templars were important," I said. "If he was Master of the Templars, surely that's something?"

"He was John's banker," Kat said dismissively. "And normally the Templars tried to keep a low profile. Yet what better way to guarantee the agreement than with his own name and a message hidden by fire in the parchment?"

This was all starting to sound ridiculous, though Kat appeared to believe it. My hand was still on her wrist, but she flicked the wheel on her lighter and a steady yellow flame emerged. She edged it closer to the vellum on my bed until, with a quick blow through pursed lips, I extinguished it like a birthday candle.

"Congratulations," she said. "I think you just spat on the Magna Carta."

Considering what she was proposing to do, that seemed trivial. Yet, to my horror, I saw that she was right and that a few drops of saliva now dotted the parchment.

I shook my head to focus on the pressing question of her pyromania. "How is it that no one has ever heard of any of this? People have been studying the Magna Carta for centuries, and in one morning you work out something that everyone else has missed?"

"You heard what Mei said: no one reads the thing. It became more important for what it symbolises than what it said. And that's perfectly logical, because the original Magna Carta doesn't make sense—unless there's more to it."

"Why is this so important to you? You could go to jail—we both could."

Kat straightened. "I haven't been entirely honest with you," she said. "My father was a historian. He wrote a book on the Magna Carta but couldn't get it published. They thought he was crazy, maybe he finally decided they were right..." Her voice trailed off.

Did she mean he killed himself? The same father who regarded life as an interruption to sleep? Or the one who had run off with her classmate, or died in a fire? None of it made any sense.

"What is it you expect to find?" I heard myself asking.

"I think Aymeric—ember—is a clue that a message was hidden using fire writing. Saltpetre was used for centuries to make fireworks and gunpowder. I think that there's a message written on the bottom inch of the parchment and that fire will bring it out. I did it myself once at school. You take saltpetre—potassium nitrate—mix it with a little water and write. When it dries it becomes invisible. If you light it, though, the trail of saltpetre burns up to reveal the message."

I was still dubious. "Even if you're right about all this, surely we should do it in some kind of laboratory?"

"If we try to go a laboratory, the first thing they'll do is put this thing back behind bulletproof glass and then no one will ever know its secret."

"You left out that we would be put behind bars," I added.

"Look," she said, "would you feel more reassured to know that we wouldn't be the first people to try this?"

"What do you mean?"

"Three hundred years ago, a guy called Sir Robert Cotton had a vast collection of manuscripts, including a copy of the Magna Carta. That's the damaged one that Cholmondeley said was now in the British Museum."

"So, someone else tried to find this fire-writing and only succeeded in damaging the parchment?"

"No. The fire got out of control and burned down the library. But it was the water that damaged the parchment. And straight afterward it was locked in the British Museum so no one could try it again."

She was so enthusiastic that I almost wanted it to be true. A more practical objection presented itself. "Smoke detectors," I said, pointing at the ceiling. "We can't do it in here or it will set off the alarm. I think I've had enough evacuations for one day."

"Fine," she said. "We'll do it on the window ledge. I smoke in my room all the time and the alarm hasn't gone off yet."

I was reluctant to touch the parchment, so she picked it up by lifting the newspaper and brought it over to the window, which I opened.

I still don't think the enormity of what she was about to do had struck me, until I watched her relight the flame and bring it down toward the empty space at the bottom of the parchment, her eyes glowing. In retrospect, I'm not sure what I had thought would happen. A line of crisp text would magically appear as an extra clause, perhaps, as if written by an invisible hand in the same cramped style? Or a dusting of smoke would see glowing letters appear, winking red on the yellowed vellum?

What actually happened was that, upon contact with the flame, a line of fire an inch high ran diagonally across the entire manuscript as light tendrils of smoke rose from it. I tried to blow the smoke out the window but only succeeded in fanning the flames, which rose higher and threatened the drapes hanging at the sides of the window. I shifted the newspaper on which the parchment rested; now smoke was getting in my eyes and causing me to cough.

"I can't see," I cried, starting to panic. The smoke alarm would go off, the parchment would be damaged beyond recognition, we would spend the rest of our lives in prison.

"But there is a message!" Kat's voice was triumphant, and more than a little relieved.

At last, the flames began to die down. Vellum itself doesn't burn very well and it was now clear that the fire had indeed been fuelled by some hidden substance on the surface. As smoke drifted out the window, I brought the parchment back inside and gasped at the result. Where once fine handwriting had recorded the details of an agreement between a king and those rebelling against him, the blackened surface left only fragments legible. And yet those blackened portions combined to form a new message in letters an inch high, scrawled across the document in a ragged hand:

CALIBURNUS IN
STANENGEM
ABSCONDETUR

With Kat's help, I brought the newspaper and its precious cargo into the room, placing it on my desk. One last ember glowed orange, then died.

A little late, the gravity of the situation began to sink in. "You realise that we've destroyed a document that had been around for eight centuries?"

"No," Kat corrected, taking out her phone to snap a picture. "We have revealed a secret that has been hidden for eight centuries: '*Caliburnus in stanengem abscondetur*'? *That* was the extra part that was missing, *that* was why they let John stay on the throne!"

"So, what does it mean?" I asked.

"I have absolutely no idea," she sighed. "But '*abscondo*' is the Latin word for hide. So, it is about something being hidden. We just have to figure out what is being hidden and where."

"'*Caliburnus*' sounds familiar." I closed my eyes, trying to remember where I had seen the word before. "It's an old name, or an alternative name for something."

It was on the tip of my tongue and I probably would have remembered it myself, but Kat had taken out her phone again. "There!" she exclaimed, holding up the screen in triumph. For the first result was the Wikipedia entry for a sword. In Latin its name was *Caliburnus,* though it was far better known by its English name, Excalibur, the legendary sword of King Arthur.

8

"This makes no sense," I said. "It's crazy."

"Why?" Kat asked. "Stories about King Arthur and Excalibur go back at least as far as the thirteenth century. Wasn't the sword thought to possess magical powers and be the key to sovereignty in Britain?"

"The stories go back much farther than that, but they're legends. Myths. Like Merlin, the Lady of the Lake, and the Round Table."

"Maybe. Or maybe some of it was true. Or maybe enough people *believed* that it was true that it didn't matter what was fact and what was fiction." Kat gestured at the newspaper on which the remnants of the Magna Carta sat. "We get enough fake news these days to understand that."

I had read enough of the stories as a kid to be interested, but also enough to know that this was bunk. "If King Arthur really did exist, he lived hundreds of years before King John. So, if he ever had a sword called Excalibur, it would have been old and rusted by the time John was on the throne.

In the stories, his sword had the power to blind enemies and its scabbard could heal wounds. That's a fable, not the description of an actual weapon."

"But the sword might not even have been used as a weapon. Maybe it was more like a symbol," Kat mused. "Even today, the King or Queen parades around with a crown, a sceptre, and an orb. Symbols of power."

"Sure." It was still impossible, but she had been right about the fire-writing. And, if I'm honest, the disappointment I now heard in her voice made me want to find a reason to believe her. "If there were a sword that established a link to King Arthur—or even to the legend of King Arthur—now that would have been something priceless."

"And to give that up," Kat continued. "That would have meant something. Not just the connection to Arthur, but the divine right to the crown."

"Giving that up would have meant giving up the claim to being above the law."

"Only he didn't give it up, did he?" Kat said. "He promised to hide it. Which means—"

"That it can be found," I finished her thought. Now I picked up my own phone and was about to google *stanengem* when there was a knock on the door.

"Huck?" It was Tshombe's voice.

"Yes, Tshombe?" I called back.

"Are you coming to lunch? It smells like carbonara, which goes bad if it sits too long." As always, Tshombe's concern for his own appetite was complemented by a concern for others.

"You go on ahead. I'll be there in a few minutes."

As his footsteps disappeared down the hallway, I wondered if he had heard Kat and me talking. "We have to tell them," I said to Kat.

"Tell who?"

"Tshombe and Mei. I understand about not going to the police until we know more, but Tshombe and Mei are different. We see them every day. I think we can trust them."

"Can't this be something between you and me?" Kat asked, putting her hand on mine.

It was tempting, to have another secret with her alone. But this felt too big. "They're like family," I tried to explain. "And in any case, I don't think I could keep something like this under wraps. It would just blurt out at some point."

"OK." Kat nodded. "I understand. But can we just tell them about the *Caliburnus* part and not how we found the message? You know Tshombe: he's afraid of his own shadow. If he finds out what we've done, he'll freak out completely."

"What *you've* done," I almost said. But theft of the Magna Carta was probably less of a crime than nearly destroying it. I nodded at the remnants of the parchment. Parts of the original Latin text were legible, but the fire had left holes in it and flakes of ash were drifting down onto the carpet. "At some point, this will have to go back to the museum."

"Of course it will," she agreed, omitting to say whether she planned to present it in person. "I never meant to steal it, only to borrow it. That argument only holds water if we can work out what the hidden message means." Now she took my hand in both of hers, massaging my fingers with her own, eyes bright once more. "If we find Excalibur, the real Excalibur, we go from being a couple of thieves to being national heroes."

"That's a fairly big 'if'," I said, though my main thought was that I didn't want her to let go of my hand. Plus, a small part of me was already imagining the tale to be true. Not necessarily Nobel Prize material, but surely some measure of fame and glory. It's amazing how quickly we can rationalise our mistakes—even mistakes yet to be made—recasting them as part of a well-thought-out plan.

For the moment, we placed the vellum back inside the newspaper, laid it flat on a shelf in my closet, and headed down to lunch. As Tshombe had warned, the carbonara had started to congeal; when we sat down, a thin line of cream on his upper lip was all that remained of his own portion.

Mei was still eating, delicately winding spaghetti around her fork and popping it into her mouth. "What happened to you?" she asked as Kat sat down. "It wasn't you lighting up a cigarette in the toilets that set off the fire alarm, was it?"

I saw Kat's eyes widen in alarm, but she recovered her composure. "No, no," she said. "I'm not that addicted."

"Good." Mei took another bite of carbonara. "Because I was just telling Tshombe here my theory about whether people are thermometers or thermostats."

"Whether people are what?" Kat's mouth was now full also, but she seemed happy to shift the topic away from our visit to the museum.

"Mei likes it when people fall into neat categories,"

Tshombe said, wiping his lip with a napkin. "It makes the world easier to understand and navigate. My father once told me a similar theory. There are two types of people in this world, he said: killers and losers." He folded the napkin and cleaned a last drop of carbonara sauce. "For myself, I do not believe in such neatness. Among other things, there are plenty of killers who are also losers."

None of quite knew how to follow that, so a few bites of pasta were taken. "It doesn't have to be neat," Mei said, picking up her thread once more. "But I do think that most people tend to be more like either a thermometer or a thermostat. Are you the kind of person who rises and falls based on what's happening around you, like a blade of grass blowing in the wind? That makes you a thermometer. Or do you set a goal and stick to it regardless of how hot or how cold it gets? Then you're a thermostat."

"I do not think that a blade of grass would serve as a very good thermometer—" Tshombe began.

"OK, forget the blade of grass," Mei said. "The question is whether you are shaped by the reality around you, or if you set your goals and then make reality fit as best you can."

"Definitely a thermostat—" Kat began, then paused as she looked up and over my shoulder.

"Is there a problem with the heating again, Miss Evershaw?" Professor Cholmondeley must have been walking past us and overheard. For a stout woman she moved very quietly.

"No, Ma'am," Kat said.

Beside the professor stood a tall, thin man wearing a black hat—I think it was a fedora. But the strangest thing about him was his stillness. Some people find mannequins uncanny because they look lifelike but don't move. Shops avoid the effect by leaving them incomplete—lacking faces, or possessed of stylised heads. This man was obviously alive, yet even his breathing did not disturb the cut of his suit. Only his eyes were in motion, flicking from person to person at the table.

Then, abruptly, he did move, breaking into a grin as the professor introduced him.

"This is Sir Michael St John," she said. "He's a lawyer and sits on Warneford's Board of Trustees."

"Sir Michael Sinjun?" I repeated.

The grin broadened; he had obviously heard this before. "It's written like 'Saint John'," he said easily, "but pronounced 'Sinjun'."

"Good God," I ejaculated. "Doesn't anybody in this country have a name pronounced the way it is spelled?" Well, in fact I didn't burst out with that. I almost did, but held back in part because of his stillness. I would like to say I had a sixth sense about him, some kind of premonition. But it was his stillness that creeped me out.

"He also sits on the Ashmolean Board," Professor Cholmondeley said. "I gather there was a bit of excitement at the museum earlier today?"

"Yes," I said. "There was a fire of some kind. We're all fine."

"Oh, that is a relief." Sir Michael St John's grin vanished as quickly as it had spread. "It would be terrible if any of you should suffer some unfortunate accident, because you were in the wrong place at the wrong time—like those awful stabbings of late." His blue eyes held mine for about two seconds longer than felt socially appropriate.

I blinked first. "That's very kind of you," I said.

"Not at all." He reached into his breast pocket and produced a name card. "If on some future occasion you are interested in another visit to the museum, I might be able to arrange a tour."

I accepted the card and looked at it. In movies, when people do a double-take, their head jerks suddenly to the side. I managed to keep my head still, but was unable to keep from my own eyes widening as I read:

Sir Michael St John
Treasurer
The Honourable Society of the Inner Temple

Mei looked over at the card as she finished another forkful of carbonara. "The Inner Temple," she said. "Isn't that the modern incarnation of the Knights Templar?"

Sir Michael smiled. "Oh goodness no. Any connection with the Templars is purely geographical. We are a mere professional association of lawyers—though I grant that we do occupy the same space that they vacated some seven hundred years ago."

"Vacated?" Mei responded. "I thought they were rounded up and arrested or executed."

"Alas, the rule of law was not then what it is now," Sir Michael sighed.

"I suppose not," Mei said. "Coincidentally, we were talking only this morning about the role of the Templars in drafting the Magna Carta. They seem to have helped lay the foundation for the rule of law a hundred years before 'vacating' the land. What a coincidence that your society occupies the same space today."

"Why yes," he conceded. "It is something of a coincidence." His body remained still and his face calm, but as he was standing next to my chair I could feel the tapping of one of his feet. "Although virtually nothing remains of the Templar buildings. Our chambers may be old"—he permitted himself a little cough—"but they are not *that* old."

"Except for the Temple Church, of course," Professor Cholmondeley said. "One of the reasons it is so wonderful to have Sir Michael on the Board is his deep knowledge of Templar Churches—an architectural style linked to our own clock tower."

"Indeed." The corners of his mouth turned up, and then back down again.

"Anyway, Sir Michael, we should get on," Professor Cholmondeley said. "The other trustees will be wondering what happened to us."

"Quite," he concurred, giving us a curt nod. "It was a pleasure."

Looking at the expression on his face, the word "pleasure" was not the first that came to mind. Yet he forced his cheek muscles up for one last, brief smile. Professor Cholmondeley waddled off, Sir Michael following close behind. If her gait resembled a duck then he was a horse, languid steps frustrated by being held to a mere trot.

"Well that was weird," I said, after they had gone. Privately,

I wondered if he was the man Professor Cholmondeley had been speaking to on the night of the storm.

"I don't buy his coincidence line for a second," Mei said, finishing her carbonara. "But what's the connection between the Templars and the clock tower?"

"The tower is the remains of an old Templar church," I said. "Professor Cholmondeley has a diagram of it in her office."

"Did she tell you why the church was demolished?" Kat asked, pulling up a website on her phone.

I shook my head.

"It was part of the purge—Friday the thirteenth and all that," she said. "Their property was seized and either handed to their rivals, the Knights Hospitaller, or destroyed. Why they left the tower standing is a mystery."

"On the architectural drawing in Cholmondeley's office there's a room below the tower, some kind of crypt," I said.

"What could be down there?" Kat asked. "If the King's men ransacked the church, it's unlikely they would have left anything valuable. Unless," she paused, "unless the crypt held the only valuable thing they wanted to keep."

"Ho, ho." Tshombe seemed to find all this amusing. "Look at the little Indiana Joneses getting ready for adventure. Sorry to disappoint you, but I got interested in archaeology myself a few years ago. Most of it is just sitting for weeks with a brush scraping dust off rocks. There is almost never a secret passageway or a puzzle leading you to hidden treasure."

Throughout the conversation, the smell of burning parchment kept coming back to me. It was only a matter of time: cameras would identify Kat as the thief; once she was traced to Warneford, I would be her accomplice. I could protest that she had done it all herself but there had been ample opportunity for me to stop her. I was as guilty as she. If there was even a chance we could work out what the puzzle meant, it was also a chance—however remote—that we might not go to prison.

"As it happens"—I tried to keep my voice calm—"I was doing a little reading and came across a puzzle of my own. A phrase that might have some connection to the Magna Carta. Do you have any idea what '*stanengem*' might mean?"

Blank stares were soon looking down at phones as we each googled for an answer, without success. "Is it Hungarian?" Tshombe asked, scratching his head.

"You said a phrase," Mei interjected. "What's the rest of it?"

Kat looked at me, but it was too late to keep quiet now.

"I think it's Latin," I began. "*Caliburnus in stanengem abscondetur.*"

Mei typed quickly on her phone and showed me the text to check the spelling. It was correct. "That's the future passive of *abscondo*," she said. "So, *Caliburnus*, whatever that is, will be hidden *in stanengem.*"

Looking at the text on her phone she frowned. "But coming after '*in*' *stanengem* is the accusative form. Like when you say in *whom* shall we place our trust. So what you should google is probably '*stanenges*' with an 's'. Try that?"

Tshombe's fingers were the fastest and he let out a low whistle. "Oh my. You're going to like this, Indiana Jones. *Stanenges* seems to be an Old English combination of *stan*, meaning stone, and some early term for gallows that lives on in the word 'hang'. I looked up *Caliburnus* also. Apparently, it is some kind of sword. The more popular name is Excalibur."

"This is fun!" Mei exclaimed. "Where did you say that this phrase came from?"

"I just"—I looked at Kat, but she shook her head—"I stumbled across it online."

Mei was still looking at her phone and frowning. "Hmm. If I search for the phrase there are no results at all. What were you reading?"

"I think it was an image file," I said quickly. "Just a fragment of text."

"Anyway," Tshombe continued. "This is something I have wanted to see for some time. Perhaps we could go on a field trip? It is not so very far away, I think."

"What isn't far away?" I pressed.

"*Stanenges*," he replied. "The stone gallows, or the stones that hang—better known as Stonehenge. That, apparently, is where Excalibur will be hidden."

9

Stonehenge was only sixty or so miles away from Oxford. That evening, sitting in the common room, we tried to work out how to get there.

Mei was looking at train schedules on her phone. "If we take the cross-country train, we can change at Basingstoke onto South Western and then connect to a bus—"

"I may be able to get us a ride," Kat said. She looked at Tshombe and squinted. "I think we'll be able to fit."

"Surely the first question," he said, "is how we get out of here? If the staff learn that we are missing without permission, they will call the police and, worse, our parents. I'm not sure about the range of these things"—he held up his wristband—"but if they contain a GPS then it won't matter if we go by train or by car."

It hadn't even occurred to me that the wristbands might be tracking devices. How could that be legal? I was about to say something, but no one else seemed bothered. Kat, for her part, focused on how to manage the threat rather than confront it. Still, I made a note in my journal about the wristbands tracking our movements.

"You leave that to me," Kat was saying. "On Saturdays we have a few hours of free time—that should be enough to go down there and back."

Tshombe nodded. "Very well. And if we do manage to get to Stonehenge, what do we do? Just ask to see the sword? If the great Excalibur were sticking out of one of those stones, I think we would have heard about it before now."

"It can't hurt to look," I said. The logical part of my brain knew that this was absurd—but that didn't mean I couldn't enjoy the possibility that it was not.

"Won't it be crowded?" Mei was now looking at visitor information. "It's getting close to the winter solstice—that means hundreds of druids and other eccentrics will be there."

"Then we'll fit right in," Kat said. "So, Saturday morning it is."

Mei put down her phone. "I don't understand. Where did this Latin text come from?"

Again, I looked at Kat. "I really can't say. I stumbled across an—an image of the Magna Carta and this phrase had been drawn on it. I think the suggestion was that this somehow supplemented the agreement with the barons. That King John had also agreed to hide Excalibur."

"I asked my father once about King Arthur," Tshombe mused. "He said it was ridiculous: no one gained power by pulling a sword from a stone. You gained it by being more ruthless than everyone else, by doing whatever it took to win. Killers and losers." He took a sip from his cup of tea. "I was eight at the time," he added.

"If Excalibur does exist, it must be extremely valuable," Mei said. "Surely someone else must have tried to find it?"

"In the legends," I said, wishing I had brought some of the books from my parents' shelves, "after Arthur's death, the sword was thrown back to the Lady of the Lake. Maybe everyone assumed that even if it did exist once, that it was lost forever."

"But instead the kings up until John kept its existence a secret?" Mei sounded sceptical.

"I agree it all sounds pretty far-fetched," I conceded, starting to wonder whether the journey was worth the hassle.

"But look on the bright side," said Tshombe. "The worst-case scenario is that we have a nice trip to the world-famous Stonehenge. And *this* time I shall take a selfie."

I read somewhere that a bad plan is better than no plan at all. Then again, as the noted philosopher Mike Tyson once observed, everybody has a plan until they get punched in the face.

Any further discussion of plans was put on hold when Tshombe leaped out of his chair with a yell. Thinking that he had sat on a tack, I shuddered at the prospect of seeing his blood. Instead he was backing away from the chair as if it were possessed.

"What's the matter?" I asked, trying to sound reassuring.

"Kill it! Kill it!" he cried.

"Kill what?" Mei asked. "The chair?"

Jaw clenched at the effort of explaining something he

clearly found obvious, he pointed to where he had been sitting.

Kat walked over to the chair, crouching down next to the armrest. "Oh, this guy?" she said lightly. "It's just a house spider. They're not particularly dangerous." She pulled a tissue from her shoulder bag and draped it over the spider, which must have been three inches across when its legs were spread. Picking it up, she moved to the window and tossed it out, holding onto the tissue. "So, you have arachnophobia too?"

After checking that the spider had not managed to cling to the tissue itself, Tshombe relaxed visibly. "I am not afraid of spiders," he said at last. "I am afraid of being bitten by one of the three dozen species with sufficient poison to cause an agonising death."

Kat dropped the tissue in a bin. "If we're going on a road trip," she said, "maybe you could inform me if there is anything else you're afraid of that I might need to know about?"

Tshombe looked at us. "Do you promise not to laugh?"

There was a pause until I jumped in. "Of course," I said, hoping that I spoke for all of us.

For a moment, he hesitated, before whispering, "Closed spaces. My father would sometimes lock me in a cupboard, then tell me that he was going to bury the cupboard in the ground."

"The fear of being buried alive is natural enough," Mei said. "It's a common image in movies, the dirt being thrown down onto you."

"And open spaces," Tshombe added. "Normally, I

am fine in most situations but wide-open spaces with no landmarks can bring on a panic attack."

"How can you be both agoraphobic and claustrophobic?" Kat asked.

"You said you were not going to make fun of me!" Tshombe protested.

"OK, OK." Kat raised her hands. "Anything else?"

He thought for another moment. "Cats."

"You're allergic?" asked Mei.

"No, I do not sneeze and my eyes do not run," he scoffed. "But I do not trust them. You know the only reason housecats do not eat their owners is that they have been bred to be small. Trust me, if you died, your cat would wait, maybe half a day—and then it would be gnawing at your face."

"Fine," said Kat. "So, heights, the dark—pardon me, serial killers hiding in the dark—fire, closed spaces, open spaces, spiders and cats. Have I left anything out?"

"Roots," he said.

"What, like the mathematical operation?" asked Mei.

"No." Tshombe shook his head. "Roots as in the part of a plant that digs its way into the ground, driving tentacles into the earth that multiply and spread. It is unnatural. And they trip you up when you least expect it."

I recalled waiting in line with him at lunch the first time we met. "Is that why you don't like carrots?"

"They are a root."

"But you're fine with potatoes," Kat challenged him. "You love chips as much as the next guy."

"Technically, they are tubers, not roots," Mei observed.

"How do you feel about parsnips?" Kat continued, but Tshombe had had enough.

"Thank you all very much for your concern," he said, "but I am going to retire for the evening and learn my lines for *Hamlet.* 'To sleep, perchance to dream' and so on."

"You know he's talking about death there, right?" Kat asked as a parting shot, before adding, "Don't forget to leave a light on—if only so you can see the spiders!"

He grimaced, considered a retort, and then left without a word. The rest of us soon followed suit, returning to our rooms to wash and prepare for bed.

The remnants of the Magna Carta remained in my closet. I left it there, but a few lingering pieces of ash had drifted to the floor. I was scooping them into an envelope when my phone rang. Mom.

"Hi, Mom," I said, putting the envelope in the closet also.

I could tell she was upset before she said a word. Maybe it was the intake of her breath on the other end. "What's wrong?"

She was composing herself, probably smoothing the skin on her forehead with the heel of her hand. Worry lines, she called them.

"Nothing," she lied. "How are you doing?"

Accomplice and arsonist. I was working through all the crimes starting with A. What was next, assault? "I'm fine," I lied in return. "I went to the museum with some friends."

"That's nice." We talked for a while about the weather, I assured her that I was eating and sleeping well. Yes, I was enjoying myself.

Finally, she got to the point. "Your father and I had a little disagreement," she said. That meant a fight.

"Oh." I tried not to sound too concerned. "What was it about?"

For five seconds she said nothing. Then: "It was about you, Huck."

"Me?" There didn't seem much else to say. Another five seconds passed.

"Your father says he feels guilty every time he looks at you. Sometimes I try to reassure him, calm him down. Other times, I think he doesn't feel guilty enough. That's when we fight."

"Guilty about what?"

Another sigh. Another five seconds. "I'm sorry," she said. "I shouldn't have brought it up—you've got enough on your plate already. I'll be fine. We'll be fine. I wanted to hear your voice, that's all." Another worry line on her forehead. "Tell me you're OK, that you're doing well?"

"I'm fine. Apart from the food and the weather this is a great holiday camp you booked me into."

She laughed. "Thanks, Huck. I'd better go. But please keep writing in your journal? I don't want to miss anything. And call or text us any time you like. OK?"

"OK," I said as she hung up.

My parents were always a little weird, but this was a new level even for them. Now that I thought about it, I did have vague memories of Dad being on the point of saying something. Hovering at the end of my bed. Then all he would say was good night.

Maybe he felt guilty about something. Maybe he wanted

forgiveness. But how was I meant to forgive him for something I didn't know he had done?

I read for a while, watched some YouTube videos, then pulled out my diary to write. As ink sank into the creamy paper, it struck me how important my journals were—not only as a record of my life, but as a way of organising it, collecting and shaping my thoughts. It's no secret that people use their phones as an extension of their brain. In the past, you had to memorise phone numbers and learn how to navigate a city; now your contact list and GPS can do all that for you. But these are all tools, the way a bicycle helps you move faster than you could run. The journals felt more like a part of me, an extension of myself.

It was approaching midnight as I wrote all this down, when my phone rang. Kat.

"Is everything all right?" I said as I picked up.

"I don't know." There was a tremor in her voice. "I'm kind of freaking out." Perhaps the prospect of a long jail term had dawned on her—the punishment for stealing a major work of cultural heritage was something I had googled between cat videos.

"Do you want to talk?" I asked.

"Can you—can you come to my room?"

I hesitated. There was no formal lights out at Warneford, but it was made clear that we were expected to be in our own rooms at night. "I'll be there in a minute."

She opened her door on the first knock. Her eyes were red. "Let me make some tea," she said. The English, I had learned, considered tea to be the remedy for all manner of problems.

I sat on the only chair as she boiled the kettle. Discounting my dream about the tower, it was the first time I had been in her room. She wore a dressing gown and the bed had been hastily remade. Her desk was a muddle of papers and books, a laptop perched atop them all. On the wall were a couple of prints. One consisted entirely of an oversized smoking pipe, below which was written "*Ceci n'est pas une pipe.*" I knew enough French to understand that it meant something along the lines of "This is not a pipe." Ha ha, *très* clever.

The act of making the tea seemed to be helping Kat relax. She took a tissue and blew her nose. "When you cry," she said, tossing it onto a pile threatening to tip out of a small wastebasket, "you should cry in the shower. That's what my mother used to say when my father was doing time in prison. Something about the hot water—it stops your eyes getting puffy. That way, people won't know you've been crying."

Her father—the boring father who may or may not have died and/or run off with a schoolmate—had spent time in prison? I let this pass. "Why have you been crying?"

She gave me my tea and sat down on the bed, her knees inches from mine.

"I'm sorry," she said. "I was being silly. I think the stress of the day has caught up with me at last." She held her cup in both hands, steam dancing around her cheeks. The redness around her eyes was fading. "Do you ever feel that you're living life at a different speed from everyone else?" she began. "Sometimes the world seems so slow, no one can keep up with you... Then, suddenly, time has raced ahead of you, a year has passed, and you can't recall living half the days that went by."

I took a sip of the tea. Peppermint. "Sure, our internal clocks rarely match up to the ones on the wall. 'Time flies when you're having fun' and all that."

She shook her head. "That's not what I mean. I mean that you're outside time itself. That your life is a series of episodes, like a TV series where every show is released at the same time. Some people are disciplined and watch once a week; others binge on the whole thing in a marathon. And some people, they dip in and out, jumping forward and backward depending on whether they like what they see."

"So, who's watching these TV shows?"

"I don't know." She sipped her own tea. "You? Me? God?"

"Maybe we could watch some episodes together," I said, moving to sit next to her on the bed, gently turning her cheek toward mine as we—

No, I only thought of that line much later. Looking back, she probably would have laughed at me if I had said it. Which is ironic, because what I actually said was: "Can I ask you something?"

"What?" Her eyes met mine. I noticed for the first time that the green irises were flecked with gold.

"I want you to promise not to laugh."

She blew on her tea and shook her head. "What is it with you guys? First Tshombe and now you. Why are men always so afraid that women will laugh at you? You know what frightens women? Not that men will laugh at us. It's that men will rape and murder us."

"I would never hurt you," I said. Some email systems enable you to retract a message after it has been sent and you have second thoughts. When someone invents that for the spoken word, I will be first in line.

"Well, that's a relief." Kat took another drink from her tea. "So, what did you want to ask me?" She put her tea down and turned to face me, our knees now almost touching. The birthmark on her throat trembled.

"I wanted to ask—"

"Yes?"

I closed my eyes, willing myself to say the words out loud and not just in my head. "I wanted to ask," I said, "if I could kiss you."

In the silence, I opened one eye, then the other. The green eyes flecked with gold never left mine, then narrowed as her hand curled into a fist and punched me hard in the stomach.

"*That's* for being so brazen," she said as I doubled over. As I tried to catch my breath to apologise she hit me again. "And *that's* for not asking me earlier." I had almost fallen out of the chair, but she moved aside so that I tumbled onto the bed next to her, following me so that our faces were next to each other. Gasping for air, I looked into her eyes in wonder as my fingers at last touched the raven black hair. "The dressing gown remains on," she said primly. "But yes, you may kiss me."

It was awkward—noses bumping, teeth colliding. It was wonderful. Time slowed, the world disappeared, for too short a moment it was only the two of us, holding each other. Holding each other together, as I realised much later.

We must have dozed off, squeezed onto Kat's single bed, her dressing gown still safely knotted—though with only a simple bow, as I saw when I woke. Her head was on my shoulder, so I lay still. From the dark outside the curtains it was still night.

I had roused from the still waters of sleep with the memory of a dream. Frustrated for want of a pen and paper to write it down, I struggled to recall the details. It was unlike any dream before or since. The gist was that my mind had somehow been transported into the body of a woman. There was nothing that really happened, just an awareness that my body felt different, that my relationship to the world and the people around me had changed. I somehow felt… closer. I was conscious of my body in an entirely different way; I felt—I felt *more.* The sensation was uncanny: everything was the same, and yet everything was different.

Beside me, I felt Kat's body shift, her arm moving to rest on my chest. I could tell by her breathing that she was awake. I ran an idle finger through her hair and was about to tell her of my dream when she spoke.

"I just had the strangest dream," she said, a languid yawn sneaking out with the words. "Somehow, my mind's eye was transported into the body of a man." I must have started, because she lifted herself up on one elbow to look at me. "What's wrong?"

I told her about my own dream. Hers was also vague and getting vaguer. I wondered aloud if one of us had spoken during our sleep, or if there might be some other explanation other than coincidence.

"Or maybe you're still dreaming now," she said, pinching my arm.

"Ow!" I protested. "If this is going to work, you're going to have to stop assaulting me."

She brought the skin that she had pinched up to her lips. "There, all better." Her desk light was still on and she squinted at me. "What's that?" she asked, pointing to my temple and reaching up to brush the hair back.

"What's what?"

"The scar." Her finger traced a line along the edge of my hair, bumping along raised skin.

There was no pain, but as I raised my own finger to touch it I knew that there must have been at some point. "A childhood injury," I said.

"What happened?"

"I—" I drew a blank. Not the way your earliest memories fade into vagueness, but the way you forget something specific, like where you put your keys. "I fell over as a kid. Blood everywhere, stitches. Lucky that my brain didn't fall out." None of that was true—or maybe it was. I had no idea, but couldn't tell her that.

It seemed to satisfy her; at least, she didn't ask any more questions. Entangled as we were, I began to wonder if part of Warneford's strategy for encouraging people to sleep in their own rooms was the impracticality of sharing such a small bed. I also didn't want to overstay my welcome.

"Are you going to be OK?" I asked.

"Sure."

"I'd like to stay, but—"

"But? But? I knew there was a 'but' coming. And

everything before the 'but' is a lie." She stood up and retrieved her tea, now cold.

"What?"

"It's how people dress up bad news: with deceit. 'I really like you, *but* as a friend.' 'I'd love to read your draft novel, *but* I'm really busy.' 'You know I love you, *but* I have to move to Mexico.'"

"OK," I said, "those all sound very specific."

"I'm sorry." She sat back next to me on the bed and put her hand in mine. "It's been a weird day."

"You can say that again."

"So, you were about to say you had to go back to your room."

"I don't want to, but—*however,* you know how they are about sleeping in your own room."

"It's fine." She kissed me again. "Go. But come back again soon?"

I lingered for another breath, then shuffled down the darkened corridor. I don't think I paid attention at the time—I wasn't noticing much of anything, to be honest—but my path would have seen me follow the green emergency lights toward the fire exit, only to turn away from it as I approached my own room.

I held up my wristband to unlock the door, lost in thought, barely feeling the paper under my feet as I entered. For the third time, it was a message constructed from cut out newspaper letters. In an age of limitless fonts on a computer, the craft of it was what I noted before even registering the substance:

The Sword is worth dying For

Now that considerably reduced the number of people who could be behind the messages. The only people who knew about the sword were Kat, Mei, Tshombe, and myself. I had just been with Kat, but I couldn't see Mei or Tshombe communicating like this. And surely, if they wanted to tell me something, they could do it directly?

I looked at the phone charging by the side of my bed. Another possibility was that our internet searches had been intercepted—there was no guarantee that Warneford's Wi-Fi network was secure. If they were tracking us through the wristbands, maybe they were reading our emails also. Yet that also seemed unlikely.

I put the note in a drawer with the other two and sat back down at my desk where the diary was still open. I had been writing about the journals as an extension of myself. I read once that writing first developed as a means of communication, sharing information between two people across distance and time. How many bushels of wheat at what price, when the army would attack, and so on. But it also became a means of expanding human memory. Committing things to paper, we no longer needed to hold them in our heads. Mrs Sellwood once told me that Socrates had opposed writing, fearing that it would make humans lazy because no one would have to remember anything. Of course, the only reason we know about this, two thousand years later, is because his student Plato wrote it all down.

The journals were more than a kind of external hard drive, however. Mrs Sellwood was right, there was something about the act of writing, a clarity that came from writing one word after another, so much neater than the messiness of real life.

I finished writing, turned off the light, and tried to sleep.

10

Ahead of us, the circle glowed red. Squashed into the car, some kind of European compact, we were stuck in tourist traffic as we attempted to leave Oxford for the motorway heading south.

Kat, now sitting in the front passenger seat, had told us to be ready to leave at nine sharp. How she planned to get to Stonehenge was a mystery until Oliver, the porter who had broken us out of the tower, drove up to Warneford's entrance. From the expression on his face he did not appear to have volunteered his chauffeuring services, but Kat had smiled at him sweetly, slipping into the front seat as Tshombe held the rear door open for Mei.

It struck me that I hadn't ridden in an actual car for a long time. In New York we mostly used the subway. Getting to the airport, we had taken a cab that seemed at least twice as big as this. And from Heathrow to Oxford there was an express bus. My leg was acting up as I tried to climb in, but with Tshombe waiting behind me I had forced myself to sit down. If he could deal with the enclosed space inside the cabin, I could manage my damn leg. He squeezed in after me and we struggled into our seat belts.

"As a child," sighed Mei, looking at the red circle, "I always wanted to be a traffic light."

"That was your ambition?" Tshombe was incredulous. "To be a lamppost?"

"Such power," she continued. "Such simplicity. Flash my red light and the world stops. The most expensive car, the most powerful truck, frozen on my command. Then change to green and everything restarts, the world in motion once more."

"I thought you guys had dancing traffic cops," I said, recalling a YouTube video that had done the rounds of social media.

"You may be thinking of the Philippines," Mei replied. "In Singapore we generally just have lights and cameras. Lots of cameras."

It was the following Saturday and we had started the drive to Stonehenge. I still doubted that we would find anything—yet, as Tshombe had said, the worst that could happen was that we might go on a nice field trip.

The morning after my midnight visit to Kat's room, I had been unsure how to behave. At breakfast, I stood uncertainly when she arrived at our table, but she simply walked up and kissed me on the lips in front of Tshombe and Mei. He gave me a pat on the shoulder as I sat down, which felt odd, but Mei busied herself with her phone and adjusting the end of her shirtsleeve. For a second, I thought she had looked a little sad. No, I corrected myself:

disappointed, as though I had let her down somehow.

Later, over coffee in the common room, we had agreed to go to Stonehenge on Saturday. I continued to parry questions about where the secret Latin text had come from. Tshombe seemed unconcerned, though Mei pressed me to recreate the search and review my browser history. I claimed forgetfulness and a right to privacy, Kat rising to my defence. Eventually, Mei let it drop.

That night, as Kat and I took a stroll around the grounds, I had observed how strange it was that there had been no news about the Magna Carta. Surely, the theft of one of English law's founding documents was worth a news story?

"You're right, it is weird," she said, lighting a cigarette, holding the flame in front of her eyes. By that point, I was inhaling so much of her passive smoke that I wondered if I could become addicted as well. "Maybe they're covering it up? Trying to avoid embarrassment over the theft?" She tried, unsuccessfully, to blow a smoke ring. "They do have three more copies. And we'll return ours once we see where this trail leads."

In the car that Saturday, the light turned green and Oliver merged onto the A34. Beside him, Kat sipped from a bottle of water. In the rear, Tshombe's head nearly touched the ceiling, alongside Mei and me in budget economy class.

Mei must have been thinking something similar. "Do you know what they used to call business class on Singapore Airlines?" she asked, shifting her handbag so that she could put her feet flat. "Raffles class. Named after Sir Stamford Raffles."

"Was he a Templar also?" Tshombe inquired.

"No," Mei replied with a laugh. "He was the colonial founder of Singapore who worked for the East India Company. How many places in the world make it so clear that, when you've arrived, you get to travel like the colonials?"

"Bah, it is not so different in my country," he said. "Our President stays in the same State House as the former colonial governors. Why should it be any different for businesspeople?" He thought for a moment. "Although I suspect that 'Rhodes Class' would be a bit of a hard sell in southern Africa."

"What about you, Huckleberry?" Kat gave me a mischievous look in the rear-view mirror. "You're being awfully quiet—America was always our favourite colony. Any legacy of Empire there?" Oliver changed lanes to pass a truck. "Oh yes, remind me: what language does your country speak?"

"Ha ha," I replied, looking at the truck as we overtook it. A line of snouts poked out the side, pigs sniffing a last few breaths of fresh air on the way to the abattoir? Beside me, Mei reached down to adjust her bag again. As she did so, her sleeve bunched up and revealed three parallel scars on her left wrist. Self-consciously, she pulled her jacket back down under her black wristband and turned toward me, but my eyes were back on the pigs. I wondered if I should say something. I probably should have.

Kat put on some music as we drove through the English countryside, oddly named towns dotting the green plains under an endless grey sky. It was late morning when she told us to look out the window and across a field.

"That's it?" Tshombe said. "It's much—"

"Smaller than you expected?" Kat finished his sentence. "Is everything in Zambia so much bigger than things here? In any case, we're some distance away. It does get a little larger."

Oliver soon pulled into a carpark near the visitor centre, the stones now hidden by a low hill. Tickets purchased, we boarded a shuttle bus with a dozen other visitors and trundled along a road now closed to traffic.

As we left the visitor centre, I looked back and saw a man emerge from a silver sports car—an old model that I recalled from a James Bond film, though the name escaped me. As he stood he appeared to stretch out, seemingly too tall to have fit in the low-slung car. Then he reached in through the open door and retrieved a black hat. Adjusting the rim, he watched our bus depart, standing so still that a pair of birds landed on the roof next to him.

I was about to say something when Tshombe cried out, "There it is!" as the monument emerged on the horizon.

The shuttle bus deposited us at a simple station where a handful of early tourists were already awaiting the return journey. Walking up the path toward the circle itself, the scale of it became more apparent—stone slabs the size of cars, delicately balanced like a child's building blocks. Oliver affected boredom, following behind us. But I saw him take out his phone to snap a photo.

"It looks like an arena," Tshombe said. "A battleground for ancient warriors, with multi-level seating for the spectators."

"There are many theories about its purpose." Mei was

reading the guide she collected at the entrance. "That's not one of them. Graveyard, druidic temple, centre for healing, astronomical calculator for predicting eclipses, and—more helpful for our purposes—a coronation place for Danish kings."

"And, as we know, something is rotten in the state of Denmark," Tshombe intoned.

"I always thought Stonehenge looked more like a giant set of wickets for cricket," Kat observed, disappointed at our reaction to what was presumably her own attempt at a joke. She turned back to Oliver, who gave a wan smile.

"I'm sure I would have laughed if I knew what wickets looked like," I said, earning an eye roll.

I was contemplating my own analogy when I bumped into Tshombe. He had stopped dead in front of me, the muscles in his neck tense to the point of stretching his jacket.

"Is everything OK?" I asked, looking to see if a spider had landed on him. Then I followed his eyes down to the ground. The path was covered in gravel, but just ahead of us gnarled wood broke the surface, the roots of a nearby tree wandering upward in their search for water.

"Wow," I said, recalling his earlier confession. "You were serious about the roots thing, weren't you?" I looked around. "Listen, unless you want Mei to slap you again, I suggest you follow me and I'll keep you away from the roots."

He didn't reply, but allowed himself to be led off the path and in a wide circle away from the offending tree. "Though this be madness," he whispered, "yet there is method in it."

"Is that more *Hamlet*?"

"Yes, Polonius in Act 2."

"Wasn't Hamlet just pretending to be mad?" I asked.

"Hard to tell," Tshombe replied. "I haven't decided yet."

We were back on the path and Mei called out to us, holding up the guide. "Oh man. We can walk near the stones, but you can only get close to them on the actual solstice—the day after tomorrow—or the equinox." She flipped over a page. "Or if you pay for a private tour."

"Ah, don't be wasting your money on that now." The man who spoke had ridden with us on the bus, a shock of white hair and beard giving him the appearance of a very surprised Santa Claus. He seemed harmless enough to me, but Mei eyed him suspiciously. He looked us over in turn, tutting under his breath as he did.

"Can we help you, sir?" I asked.

Oliver, our chaperone, was out of earshot and typing something on his phone. He glanced up at us and then returned his attention to the screen.

"No, as a matter of fact I was wondering if I can help *you*," the old man replied, scratching his beard. "You all look like you've lost something and don't even know what it is you're looking for. And don't be calling me 'sir'. My name's not 'sir'."

"I'm sorry, uncle," Mei said, ever polite to her elders. "What is your name?"

He straightened. "It's Arthur," he said. "Arthur Uther Pendragon, if you want to be all formal about it."

"Uther Pendragon," I repeated. "As in the father of King Arthur?"

"Indeed," he said proudly. Then shrugged. "Well, that's after I got it changed by deed poll. Before that, I was Thomas Bowett. But my license and everything now says Arthur Uther Pendragon. It's here somewhere." He began looking through his pockets, causing a series of small items and a half-eaten sandwich to fall out.

"That's quite OK," I assured him. "So, I'm guessing you know these stones well?"

"Oh yes, I've been coming here for years. Fighting the bastard government to let us near the blessed stones. It's my religion, I argued. Went all the way to the European Court of Human Rights!" As he spoke, his eyes drifted across the stones and then up toward the clouds.

"Did you win?" Tshombe asked.

The old man's eyes dropped to the ground. "No," he said. "Bastard government did. But then their Lordships decided that this was a public highway after all, so we get to gather on the solstice for our rituals and what not. So, I still says I won."

I bent down to pick up a set of keys that had fallen on the grass next to the trail and passed them to him. "What happens at this solstice?"

He brightened. "We gather, we sing, we celebrate the return of the sun. You know that the winter solstice is the day when the days stop getting shorter and start getting longer. So, it symbolises life, rebirth." He lowered his voice so we had to lean in to hear him. "*That's* why the Christians chose it as the birthday of their baby Jesus."

He pocketed the keys and we continued walking along the path around the stones. "You should come back on

Monday, on the winter solstice! Make sure you're here early. You want to get in before some of the crazies arrive, and before there's been too much drinking." He paused to regard the monument, his voice deepening and arms rising as if he spoke to a larger group. "When the sun rises at eight minutes past eight, you get the full majesty of Stonehenge on display." His arms fell to his sides. "Unless it's cloudy or raining, in which case it'll be pretty miserable."

"What time did you say the sun rises?" I asked.

He scratched his beard again. "As I recall, it's eight minutes past eight o'clock. Easier to remember than the summer solstice, when the sun comes up at the ungodly hour of four fifty-two. Only the true believers make it here for that one—and by god we deserve a good stiff drink then." He patted another pocket and produced a small hipflask, giving us a wink as he took a swig. Then he offered it around to us, a stray white whisker clinging to the rim. We politely declined.

I looked at the others to see if they had made the same connection. Tshombe looked confused. "The clock tower?" I whispered. "Stuck at eight-oh-eight?" His eyebrows rose.

"And what happens when the sun rises?" Mei asked.

"I was about to tell you, if you'd let me finish." He replaced the hipflask and shook his head, in the process dislodging a crumb from his beard. I noticed that a few birds had been following us, beaks darting to the ground to pick up bits of food left in his wake. "At eight minutes past eight, the sun rises on the winter solstice. Now in summer, when you stand inside the circle, the solstice sun rises directly over the Heel Stone." He pointed toward a lumpy stone outside the circle, standing about sixteen feet high. "But in winter, the tallest stone in the field, Stone 56—by gum, you'd think they could have given it a better name than that, wouldn't you?—anyway, Stone 56 points straight at the sunrise. Or rather," once again he lowered his voice, as if worried about being overheard, "it would have, if they'd not botched a repair done a century ago. The fools straightened the stone and set it in concrete. Made everything nice and symmetrical—but the world ain't symmetrical, is it? So now the stone points straight up like a beanpole. That's what they should call it, not Stone 56, but beanpole."

He picked at his beard, prying something out with his fingernails that he debated eating before flicking it onto the ground. "Maybe I'm being a little harsh," he conceded. "They worried that it would eventually topple over, what with the stone it had been leaning on being stolen hundreds of years earlier."

"Stolen?" Mei said. "I read that over the thousands of years a few of the stones had disappeared, but who do you think stole them?"

"Stones like this don't wear away and disappear," he said. "It's possible, I grant you, that some of the gaps are just gaps, and some was taken for building by the villagers. But this one was definitely stolen."

"By whom?" Kat's interest was now piqued also.

He looked up to the clouds where a sliver of sunlight now poked through. The sight of it seemed to cheer him. "It was those bastard Christians, wasn't it? The stone that the rising sun kisses on baby Jesus' birthday—the winter solstice. Seven hundred years ago, they took it for their church."

"Priests came and stole a twenty-five-ton stone?" Mei asked.

"Not priests." The old man scoffed at the thought. "Imagine them in their cassocks and vestments and whatnot trying to haul one of these blighters." He chuckled, before turning serious. "No, they sent the army for a job like this. 'Soldiers of Christ' they called themselves. You know, the ones who fought the Crusades and whatnot. Then, after the Muslims got themselves organised and pushed the bastards out of the so-called Holy Land, they came to places like this to steal from folks that couldn't defend themselves."

Again, he busied himself with his beard, eventually extracting what appeared to be part of a potato crisp. He popped it in his mouth.

As he chewed, I saw Mei's expression change as she made the same connection as me. "Do you mean," I said slowly, "that the stone was taken by the Knights Templar?"

He nodded. "Those are the bastards!"

"And they took it to their church in London?" Kat asked.

"No, no. Bastards were too lazy for that," he shook his head, as if the memory of the crime were still fresh. "They took it to one much closer," said the man who called himself Arthur Uther Pendragon. "They took it to their church in Oxford."

11

In the front of the car, Oliver steered with one hand, affecting boredom once more. The rest of us sat in silence, turning our heads for a last glimpse of the circle of rocks—a monument to a forgotten people's hopes for the future, and our own incomplete window into the past.

After a couple more questions and some further rambling about the "bastard government", Arthur Uther Pendragon had shuffled off, a pair of birds trailing him. We completed our circuit of the stone formation, Tshombe took selfie after selfie until he was satisfied, and then we reboarded the bus.

Mei had insisted on learning what we could from the visitor centre, but its focus was largely archaeological. Speaking to a couple of the guides, I got the impression that they regarded most of the past few centuries as essentially current affairs. They did acknowledge that Stone 56 had been moved and straightened in restoration works done in 1901, but dismissed any suggestion that another stone had been stolen. A gentle question about King Arthur was pooh-poohed as a child's fable, reminiscent of stories crediting the creation of Stonehenge to the wizard Merlin and a helpful giant. The guides preferred an account that stressed the role of logs greased with animal fat.

At Tshombe's request, we bought lunch in the café. This consisted of an inexplicable mix of cheese and pickles between bread that was more seed than dough. I don't know what ploughmen did to offend the English, but apparently this sandwich was their punishment. There was no sign of the black-hatted man I had seen earlier, nor his silver sports car. I began to wonder if I had imagined his resemblance to Sir Michael.

But Kat's theory no longer seemed quite so crazy. I waited until Oliver went to the café's bathroom before raising it with the others: "What if the Templars did more than just help King John? We know that they were his bankers. But what do banks do when you get in trouble, if you can't pay back your debts?"

Tshombe stopped reviewing the photographs on his phone and pondered my question. "They take you to court, or they threaten you."

"Or they claim whatever you put up as collateral." It was Kat who spoke, taking my hand. Was that because she was excited about the mystery, or because Oliver was out of sight?

Mei looked up from her own phone, her brow creased into a sceptical frown. "You think that King John took out a mortgage on Excalibur?"

"I agree, it sounds odd," I conceded. "But look at what

we know: he was weak, the Templars were bankrolling him, the Barons had him at their mercy, and whatever he gave up in 1215 made it possible for kings to be held accountable to rules down here on Earth."

"And what he gave up was Excalibur, a magical sword?" Mei asked. "Which he stuck back in a rock here at Stonehenge—though no one appears to have noticed or mentioned it until the Templars decided to pilfer it, together with a piece of bluestone bigger than a car, and bury it below a building that happens to be about a hundred metres from where we are staying?"

"Now that you put it like that—" I began.

"Exactly!" Tshombe exclaimed. "That's exactly what happened."

"Then," Mei continued, still tapping on her phone, "after the Templars take control of Excalibur and its stone, they contrive to be persecuted and disbanded, while the building in which they stored the sword is demolished?"

"Hmm." Tshombe sucked his lower lip. "I agree that this requires further thought." Then he clapped his hands together. "Unless it is like that Kevin Spacey film in which the Devil's greatest trick is convincing the world that he doesn't exist. What if the Templars only *pretended* to be disbanded—what if they hid themselves so they could retain power but operate in the shadows. What if—"

"What if they secretly controlled the throne and thereby the British Empire?" Mei offered. "Then they established Freemasonry to control the United States and *its* empire, all the while retaining a stranglehold on global finance through the Rothschild family. Don't forget that

'Rothschild' means 'red shield', which recalls the red cross of the Templar logo. Oh, and they also murdered JFK and caused 9/11. Plus, the moon landings were faked."

"Now you are making fun of me," Tshombe said, crossing his arms.

"No, no," Mei protested, putting her phone away. "But that is literally what you get if you google 'crazy Templar conspiracy theories'."

We sat without speaking, each lost in our thoughts. I took out my journal to make some notes. "You have to admit," I said, "the link with the tower is pretty bizarre. Right down to the clock being frozen at exactly the time that the sun rises at Stonehenge on the winter solstice."

"Maybe it's actually stuck at eight past eight in the evening," said Mei. But she didn't sound convinced.

"And all through term there has been some kind of construction work going on in the tower." Kat flashed me a look. This had been something just between the two of us, but it seemed pointless to exclude Mei and Tshombe.

As it turned out, Mei knew anyway. "I thought they were reinforcing the tower, trying to make it safer."

"In secret? In the dead of night?" I asked. "Maybe. Or maybe Professor Cholmondeley and Sir Michael—that lawyer from Inner Temple—are looking for something in the tower also. There's one way to find out."

Tshombe grinned. "Excellent!" he said. "Another field trip. I am beginning to like these field trips."

Further discussion had been cut short when Oliver returned. As he did, I felt Kat's hand slip out of mine. How did she talk him into driving us out here? When he helped us out of the tower, he had said that they were even. What did she have over him now? I wasn't sure I wanted to find out.

Later, driving back to Warneford, she sat in the front seat beside him once more, occasionally whispering something that made him smile. Was that meant to make me jealous? It was working.

Then I saw that Oliver was looking repeatedly in the rear view mirror, before changing lanes suddenly.

"Everything all right?" I asked.

Eyes still on the road, his lips were pursed. "I think we're being followed," he said. "A car has been behind us since shortly after we left Stonehenge."

"Is it a silver sports car? An old one?" I turned to look myself.

"Yes, an Aston Martin," Kat replied, a hint of suspicion in her voice. "How did you know?"

"Near the visitor centre I saw someone who looked like Sir Michael getting out of a car like that."

"Why didn't you say anything?"

I hesitated. "Er, I didn't want to freak you guys out?"

"Well then, mission accomplished," Kat said.

Beside me, Mei whispered, "Sarcasm?" I nodded.

"What we should do," Tshombe said, "is get to some traffic lights and then wait until they are about to turn red. Then at the last minute we race through the intersection and cars coming from the side will block him in." He grunted in disappointment. "But there are no traffic lights on this motorway. Can you find a railway line, where we can cut across the tracks just as a locomotive arrives pulling a great many carriages? Then, after he waits for them to pass, we will be long gone."

"Or how about we slam on the brakes, spin the car, and drive into the oncoming traffic?" Kat asked. "He'd have to be mad to follow us then." As Tshombe weighed up this possibility, Kat added, "Yes, Mei, that was sarcasm also."

We continued on the A34 to Oxford. Oliver varied the car's speed, but the silver Aston Martin never overtook us or fell too far behind. Not many cars were on the road. When I paid attention, however, I saw that a good number were also broadly keeping pace with us, overtaking the occasional truck.

At last, we turned off for the Oxford Ring Road and I craned my neck to see the silver car with its gangly passenger stay on the highway toward the Midlands. Oliver also watched through the rear-view mirror.

"It's possible that it was my imagination," he said as we approached Warneford.

"And mine also?" I replied. "That seems hard to credit."

We turned into the driveway leading to the small drop-off area by the main entrance.

"Well, I do not think I am imagining *that*," Tshombe said, pointing directly ahead of us. For in the middle of the driveway stood the small but imposing form of Professor Cholmondeley.

Oliver sighed and pulled into a short-term parking lot, next to a warning about cars that overstay being subject to wheel clamps. A single beckoning finger summoned us, after which the professor turned on her heel and went into the building. We followed into her office, which already had extra chairs so the five of us could be seated.

"In the six years that I have run this programme," Professor Cholmondeley began, sitting down behind her desk, "I have tried to rely more on good sense than on rules. If we are to prepare our young men and women to enter the community, we need them to act based on what they feel is right—not merely to avoid punishment." She paused to realign some of the files on her desk. "On days like today, I wonder if that approach has not been a mistake."

"It was the weekend," I said. "We decided to take a trip into the countryside."

"A field trip," added Tshombe.

"You, of all people," Professor Cholmondeley continued, eyes fixed on Oliver, "should have known better than to take residents off site without a word."

"Yes, Ma'am." Oliver bowed his head.

"I didn't think we needed to ask permission to leave Warneford," Kat protested.

"You didn't think," the professor repeated, nodding. "That much, at least, is true. You have to remember that I have a responsibility here for all our residents, and to those that care for them." Her eyes moved to each of us in turn. "And I cannot fulfil that responsibility if I do not know where you are."

Her tone was an odd mix of concern and anger. Yet I couldn't for the life of me understand why she was so worked up about us going on a drive. We had missed no classes or activities. We were back safely. I was about to say as much when Kat spoke again. "I'm sorry, Dr Cholmondeley. It won't happen again."

I turned to look at Kat, wondering why she had given in so easily. As I did, I glanced out the window and saw a silver sports car—an Aston Martin—heading toward the reserved lots for staff.

"You have a responsibility to your trustees also, don't you?" I inquired, returning my attention to the professor.

"Of course I have a responsibility to the trustees," she said impatiently. "But they know that the wellbeing of our residents is the same as the wellbeing of Warneford." The phone on her desk rang. "Very well," she said, dismissing us. "That will be all. As for you"—she pointed a finger at Oliver—"I shall deal with you later."

As we stood to leave, I saw that the architectural drawing of the tower no longer hung by the door. The phone rang a third time. "A shame," I said innocently, gesturing toward the empty space on the wall, "I liked that drawing."

The professor picked up the phone but cupped her hand over the mouthpiece. "Really?" she said. "I was beginning to find it quite tiresome myself. You may go." She waited until we were outside before lifting the handset to her ear.

"Wow," I said as the door closed, leaving the five of us in the hallway. "That was weird."

Kat apologised to Oliver, who shrugged. "I'll be fine," he said. "But I'm done with favours, OK? Now I've got to go move the car or else my brother porters will take great joy in clamping it."

She nodded as he left.

Tshombe clicked his tongue. "That woman is more highly strung than a trapeze," he observed. "Maybe she should take a field trip herself."

"Plus," I added. "You'll never guess what car just pulled up outside."

"Was it a silver Aston Martin?" Mei asked.

Before I could reply, the loping figure of Sir Michael St John appeared at the other end of the corridor. "Why hello!" he declared, removing his hat in a fluid movement as he approached. "What a pleasure to catch up with our four musketeers once again—or would you prefer to be the four horsemen of the apocalypse?"

"The pleasure is ours, Sir Michael," I replied as he approached. "What brings you back to Warneford so soon?"

"Oh, just some tedious administrative matters." He waved his hand as if shooing away a fly. "Paperwork and so on. I shouldn't complain, really. Paperwork is what keeps the legal profession in business, eh?" He chuckled to himself.

"And what would we do without lawyers?" I asked.

"Ha ha." The chuckle died out. "Quite."

"Since you're here," I said, "perhaps we can take advantage of your other expertise."

He was next to us now and paused, inclining his head politely to listen. Even now, his stillness unsettled me.

"The other day, Professor Cholmondeley mentioned that you were knowledgeable about Templar churches," I continued, "like the one our clock tower was once a part of."

"Yes." His jaw was the only part of his body that moved.

Beside me, I felt a nudge from Kat, but I didn't want to miss the opportunity to question him. "I was reading about these churches and how they sometimes have underground chambers—crypts, I think they're called. And I wondered what sort of things might be stored in these crypts."

Sir Michael remained still for a few seconds, then inclined his head further to examine the rim of his hat, running his fingers along the felt edge. "It's hard to say," he said at last. "Typically, crypts were the place in which coffins, or sarcophagi, were stored. Sometimes religious relics might be displayed as well."

Mei listened to this, chewing on her lower lip. "It's funny, though, that the word stem, 'crypt', has a very different meaning—that of hiding something, as in cryptic or cryptography."

He turned to look her in the eye. "I suppose that's true. Certainly, some churches have been known to store valuable items in their crypts that they didn't want to be seen—or which they thought *should* not be seen." Again, he stood without movement, before extending his wrist to regard an expensive silver watch. "I fear, however, that any further dalliance with all of you will delay me from my next appointment. Therefore, I bid you adieu." He gave a kind of nod, then headed on past Professor Cholmondeley's door and down the corridor.

"Should we follow him?" Tshombe asked.

"Even if he goes straight to the tower," Kat said, "I doubt he's going to open the door and invite us in."

"And if there is a twenty-five-ton piece of bluestone beneath the tower that has been buried there for hundreds of years," Mei added, "I don't think it's going anywhere."

Tshombe was clearly disappointed. “Then how are we going to get into this crypt?”

“The porters have the key,” I said, looking at Kat. “Any chance your pal Oliver might lend it to us?”

Kat made a face that I couldn’t quite decipher. “Let’s discuss that later. First, let me run an errand. I’ll see you all at dinner.” She started toward the door, turning back almost as an afterthought to give me a quick kiss on the cheek.

I was still getting used to such public displays of affection, my face reddening only slightly on this occasion. Tshombe seemed pleased at our relationship; Mei either didn’t notice or pretended not to.

We went our different ways and the afternoon drifted by as I read, did a load of laundry, and tried to find out more about the background of Sir Michael St John. An Oxford graduate—naturally—he was a patron of the arts and a generous supporter of mental health and other causes. The Inner Temple website included a glowing biography and there were various appearances in the newspapers about some high-profile cases. Even his opponents in court spoke highly of him.

Heading into dinner that evening, I was ready to concede that we might have been too quick to judge Sir Michael. It was Saturday night and hamburgers were on offer—or at least the English approximation of hamburgers. Having once got into a heated argument over the alleged German origins of the dish, I knew not to complain. I also knew to avoid what the English called mustard, a paste clearly designed not to add flavour so much as to kill the taste buds that might detect it.

Tshombe was there early, giving him a better chance of second or third helpings. Kat had sent a text message that she was running late, so I joined Mei in the queue while Tshombe negotiated for his preferred burger ahead of us.

"Did you ever notice," I said as we swiped our wristbands at the counter, "that there are no chains of English restaurants around the world? You have French, Spanish, Italian, and so on—not to mention all the Asian cuisines—but not English."

"National labels can be a bit misleading," she replied. "I saw a store in London selling something called 'Singapore noodles'. I can tell you that no such thing exists in Singapore. I think it might be Cantonese."

As I began assembling my burger, she took half a bun and the smallest piece of meat.

"Huck," she said, stocking up on lettuce. "What do you want to get out of your time here?"

"That's a weird question," I replied, though it was one I still struggled to answer. What I mainly wanted was a straight answer as to why I had come here in the first place. "I mean, education is all about expanding opportunities, pushing your limits. Transformation and all that."

"What about self-improvement? Preparing yourself for the world? Bettering yourself?"

"Yes, that also." I squirted some ketchup into a small circle on the patty. "What about you, why are you here?"

"I think I'm more like Tshombe," Mei answered.

"What do you mean?"

She passed on the ketchup but spread a bold amount of mustard on her bun. "I wish I wasn't so afraid all the time."

"Afraid? Afraid of what?"

Mei's fingers reached to her left sleeve, the sleeve that hid scars on her wrist that were too straight to be accidental. She was about to say something when her phone rang. Excusing herself to answer it, her back straightened as she did. I couldn't see her face, but it was clearly not good news.

"What's wrong?" I asked when she came back, helping her with the tray.

"That was the Singapore Embassy," she said, a faint quaver in her voice. "They said my parents were in an accident and I should fly home immediately. They've asked Dr Cholmondeley to have one of the porters drive me to the airport."

"I'm so sorry. Are they in the hospital?"

"It was a car crash. They're both unconscious. There's a flight at ten tonight that I can take." Her face was troubled, but she was also planning, working out what she needed to pack in the time remaining.

"Do whatever you need to do. I'll explain to the others."

We had reached our customary table, where Tshombe sat contemplating his burger. "Explain what?"

Mei looked to be at the point of tears. I put a tentative hand on her shoulder. "She needs to fly back to Singapore. Her parents were in a traffic accident."

"Go," Tshombe said. "Nothing is more important than family. I may hate my father and all that he did to make my childhood a therapist's hunting ground. But if he needs me, I will be there. And, when it is time for him to pass, I will stand next to him, holding his hand until the son of a bitch croaks out his last bitter breath."

"That's—very sweet of you," she said uncertainly. She looked at me. "Um, tell Kat I said goodbye."

"Sure."

My hand was still on her shoulder. She put her other hand on top of mine and looked me in the eye. "And, don't do anything stupid while I'm gone?"

"Of course," I replied without thinking. That was unfortunate because, if I had thought about it, I might have asked what she meant.

We had still not sat down. Mei now glanced at her small hamburger, then pushed the plate in front of Tshombe, nodded, and left.

Tshombe and I ate in silence for a few minutes, other students collecting their food and discussing the day. At one end of the hall I saw Professor Cholmondeley enter and then leave again, looking for someone.

Then I smelled the familiar fragrance of perfume and burnt tobacco. "Well, if it isn't Tweedledum and Tweedledummer," Kat said, dropping her shoulder bag next to my backpack and sitting down. Her plate had a hamburger patty wrapped in lettuce but no bun. The latest of her periodic diets was to exclude carbohydrates from the menu. I wasn't a big fan of the English approach to burgers, but surely this was a threat to the category itself.

She rearranged the lettuce to lift up the patty and took a bite. "Where's Mei?" A dribble of juice started to make its way down her chin.

I told her about the accident and Mei's sudden trip home.

Kat put down her lettuce-burger. "She must feel terrible. I'll try to catch her before she leaves."

We continued eating, each in our own thoughts. Our plates were almost empty when there was a rap on the head table as Professor Cholmondeley rose to speak.

"Ladies and gentlemen," she began. "It is always a delight to welcome back our distinguished board member and supporter, Sir Michael St John." He sat beside her, but even with the professor standing in modest high heels their heads were level. "As you may know, Sir Michael has a strong personal connection to Warneford. With the festive season approaching, I thought I would take the opportunity to ask him to say a few words to our little community. Sir Michael?"

Professor Cholmondeley sat down as her guest unfolded himself to stand up. He looked around the room, taking out a piece of paper from an inside pocket, glanced at it briefly, then replaced it.

"Thank you, Dr Cholmondeley," he said graciously before addressing the room as a whole. "As you may know," he began, "the origins of what we now call psychology tended not to be very scientific. One sees a hint in the name itself, for psychology literally means study of the *psyche*—the Greek word for 'soul'. The Bible is full of stories of individuals possessed by demons, at least some of whom might have been more properly diagnosed as suffering from schizophrenia rather than the ministrations of Beelzebub. In the Middle Ages, deviant behaviour was often blamed on witchcraft: an alleged practitioner might be bound and flung into a lake—if she sank, she was innocent but would probably drown; if she floated, she was a witch and would be burned."

He allowed himself a wry smile. "I myself am not trained in psychology, but I have learned how valuable modern diagnoses and treatments can be. Rigorous scientific method has, if anything, shown us how 'normal' abnormality can be. According to the World Health Organisation, up to one-third of us can expect to experience some kind of disorder in our lifetime, with the most common being anxiety and depression. That is why the work that you are doing here is so important. Communities like yours—like ours—at Warneford, through education and training, can help address the greatest problem in treating such disorders: the stigma associated with admitting that one has a problem in the first place."

Turning to look at the professor, he invited her to stand once more. "That is why, in support of the magnificent work Dr Cholmondeley and her colleagues are doing here, my family is pleased to be launching the Mary St John Mental Health Awareness Fund. This fund, named in honour of my mother, will support outreach by Warneford and its ongoing clinical programmes to bring mental health support to the community in Oxford and beyond."

He paused, beaming, until Professor Cholmondeley led a smattering of applause. We joined in half-heartedly. "In addition," he said, "my family is proud to be supporting restoration of the medieval clock tower that is Warneford's most distinctive architectural feature. After an extensive study, we are providing it with new foundations. The exterior should remain untouched, but this will ensure that our beloved tower continues into this new millennium on a firmer footing." Again, he paused, though it was only the professor who laughed at his joke. "Who knows," he added, "we might even get the clock to tell the time every now and then." This earned a murmur of amusement that echoed through the hall.

Professor Cholmondeley thanked him and dessert was served. They continued chatting, her animated, him unsettlingly still, until they departed together.

Watching them leave, Kat suggested an evening walk—code, I knew, for her having a cigarette. Tshombe said he had a rehearsal to go to; that might have simply been an excuse not to be a third wheel. The two of us took our coats and headed out to the grassy meadow within Warneford's grounds.

"Let's not go too far," she said. "I heard that a third student was stabbed not far from here. The police think it's the same person behind the attacks but have no idea who it is. All the victims were drunk or didn't see it coming. But the media are starting to call him the modern Jack the Ripper."

The night was still, our footsteps on the gravel path the only sound. We walked arm in arm, her other hand trailing tendrils of smoke.

"Do you think about the future?" I asked, recalling my brief conversation with Mei.

Cigarettes are a useful way of buying time to think, I had discovered, and Kat now used hers to full advantage. "Long-term planning was never my strong suit," she replied, exhaling. "If it were," she added, "I probably wouldn't smoke."

I had been contemplating about asking her to quit. Part of me was concerned that, if she was forced to choose between cigarettes and me, I might come second. "Do you want to stay in Basingstoke?"

Kat laughed at that. "Good God, I hope not," she said. Then she put on a stern voice: "So, Miss Evershaw, where do you see yourself in five years?" Another drag on the cigarette, before she answered her own question. "I honestly don't know. With my parents gone, there's nothing tying me down."

She had said that she was joking, clinging to her teddy bear as the house burned down, flames consuming her childhood. She had said a lot of things. "Your parents," I asked, "they really did die in a fire?"

The embers glowed as she drew another smoky breath, exhaling as she nodded.

I pulled her closer to me. "I'm so sorry."

"It was a long time ago," she said. "I was a kid. Some kind of electrical fault. I bounced around foster homes and schools, somehow ending up here."

"Do you think you could ever leave England?"

"And go where?"

I hesitated. But this felt right, being with Kat felt right. "The United States? New York, maybe?"

There was a catch in her step. She ground out the embers of the cigarette under her heel, turning to face me as the moon peeked out from behind the clouds. "Oh Huck," she said. "I know I can be a bit of a cow, but I'm so glad that I met you."

"And everything before the 'but' is a lie, right?" I

quipped, raising a hand to move a stray lock of hair from her cheek.

She looked down at the ground. "Just be careful? I sometimes worry that I hurt the people I care about the most." Her eyes met mine and I saw that they were welling with tears. "I never mean to, but I usually find a way to mess things up."

"That's OK," I said, holding her close. "I like messy." Then, by the light of the silvery moon, we kissed. And though I know it's a cliché, as our lips met I heard angels singing—until I realised that it was a small band of Christmas carollers rehearsing nearby. The kiss, the music, the moonlight was as perfect a moment as I could imagine. Even now, despite everything, the thought of it brings warmth to my chest, the filling of a void that I didn't even know existed.

On the walk back, I truthfully could not feel my feet. It was cold, to be sure, yet I no longer sensed the gravel under my shoes.

Then a noise in the bushes made us both freeze.

A hedge ran alongside the path. From within it came the rustle of something pushing against leaves and small branches. A body stretching itself out, pressing through the foliage. Kat had heard it also. Almost certainly, it was nothing—our imaginations acting up because we had been discussing the stabbings. Jack the Ripper indeed. Should we run?

I turned on my phone's flashlight and shone it into the bushes—either to see what was in them, or else to blind them temporarily. "Hello?" I called, willing my voice to sound more confident than I felt. "Is there anyone there?"

The movement stopped as the carollers finished the last verse of a song. Our vaporous breaths were the only sound; I could also feel my heartbeat in my ears. I tapped Kat on the shoulder and pointed down the path in the direction of Warneford. She nodded and was about to take a step when an explosion of black erupted from the bushes.

I stifled a scream, but beside me Kat was laughing. "Poor little fella," she was saying. "I'm pretty sure we scared him more than he scared us."

I wasn't so sure about that, yet I followed her eyes to where a black cat was scampering off the college grounds. "Oh man," I exhaled, before laughing also.

We returned to Warneford proper. As we approached our rooms, Kat whispered in my ear to give her time to shower and brush her teeth. "Then come to my room and give me a goodnight kiss?"

I promised to do so. Instead of going to my own room immediately, I walked up to the common room. It was empty. Looking across the quadrangle, the tower was dark.

On a whim, I took out my phone and pulled up Mrs Sellwood's contact details. Her email and cellphone no longer worked, but I still had her office number. It was Saturday afternoon in New York and the office would still be open, but I didn't know if she was rostered on. There was only one way to find out.

As the number rang, I wondered what to tell her. She had always assured me I would find love, that I deserved to be happy. Now that I thought I might be experiencing those emotions it felt natural to want to share them with her. She had done so much for me.

"Hello?" The voice was unfamiliar and sounded uncertain.

"Is that Mrs Sellwood's office?" I asked.

"Uh—sorry, the receptionist stepped out so I promised to answer the phone. I'm just here doing an internship." The man sounded barely older than I was.

"That's OK," I said. "I was hoping to speak with Mrs Sellwood if she's available."

"Who?"

I spoke more clearly in case there was a problem with the line. "Mrs Sellwood."

There was silence on the other end of the line. I was about to repeat the name a third time when the voice responded. "Um, sir, I'm very sorry to inform you that Mrs Sellwood was killed about two months ago."

That made no sense. It was before I left New York. I only missed saying goodbye because I was so short of time.

"Are you sure?" I asked, repeating her name, knowing how stupid I sounded and not caring.

"I'm very sorry," the intern said again.

I had to keep him on the line. "You said she was killed? By whom?"

"Ah, sir, perhaps you should call back when the normal receptionist is here?"

"By whom?" I pressed.

Now he was quiet. "Well, it's all public anyway," he began, at first speaking to reassure himself. "She was stabbed by one of her patients."

12

I hung up the phone and walked back in the direction of my room. How had I not heard about Mrs Sellwood's death? I might not have been a blood relative, but we had known each other for years and she was closer to me than anyone other than my parents. Sometimes closer than them.

Truth be told, we did argue occasionally. But all relationships have their ups and downs. It was unfortunate that our last argument had also been our last meeting. I can't even remember what we argued about. I do remember raising my voice, though. I regretted it at the time—all the more now that I knew those were my last words to her.

Even so, someone should have told me. I would have gone to the funeral, expressed my condolences to her family and all that. Because she must have had a family.

"Huck, are you all right?" Professor Cholmondeley was at the other end of the corridor, walking toward me.

"Yes, thank you," I replied, trying to navigate past her.

She intercepted me, stout frame blocking the way. "I've

been meaning to speak with you," she began, "about a delicate subject. Walk with me?" She set off before I could reply. After weighing the alternative, I followed, stooping so that our heads were level.

"Huck," she said, turning a corner, "I know you've been spending a lot of time with Miss Evershaw—Kat. That in itself is not a problem. At Warneford we encourage all our residents to form friendships. More, uh, intimate relationships, however, are generally *not* encouraged. We do understand that you are nearly adults and deserve to be treated as such. Yet, given the vulnerable position of some members of our community, there is a considerable risk of"—she searched for the right word—"misunderstanding."

The hallways were empty, though she spoke in a low voice. "I am not, I should stress, one of those who think that love is impossible in these circumstances." Her voice took on a different tone, as if recalling something from her own days as a student. "Aristotle thought that love is a soulmate who serves as a mirror in which we might see our better selves. If that other person is so different from us that they cannot function as a mirror, then there can be no love. I happen to think that Aristotle was wrong about that."

What on earth was she talking about? I wondered. I knew the English were a bit repressed about sexuality, but this was ridiculous. The professor herself seemed to recognise that she was rambling and needed to get to the point.

"What I mean to tell you, Huck," she continued, "is that it is a fine thing that you are making friends here. Mei and Tshombe, in particular, are good influences—and I think that you are having a positive impact through your friendship with them."

But—there was a "but" coming.

"But Miss Evershaw has been going through an extremely difficult stage." We reached the college entrance, where she paused. Neither of was dressed for the drizzle coming down outside. "I gather that she has become obsessed with the Warneford clock tower, making up all sorts of stories about what is, in fact, a fairly unexciting architectural relic. It has some historical significance and a certain charm, I suppose. Yet she has taken it upon herself to construct some kind of conspiracy theory around this relic.

"I am concerned," she concluded, "that your relationship with her is becoming unhealthy, and that the tower might pose a risk to you both."

And there it was. "So," I summarised, "stay away from Kat, and stay away from the tower?"

She looked out the window, before turning to me. "Normally, I prefer not to meddle in residents' social circles or deny their curiosity. But I fear in this case I must insist."

"You must insist?" I repeated back to her. Outside, I could see Sir Michael's Aston Martin still parked in its lot. "Or what?"

She seemed not to hear the question. "Huck, I am telling you this for your own good. I blame myself, really. When Kat requested to be put in your group, I agreed. She had been making real progress; as a second year, as an Englishwoman welcoming foreign guests, I thought it would be positive for her to take on some responsibilities. Unfortunately, I was wrong."

I had had enough. "Thank you, Professor," I said, preparing to leave. "This has all been very interesting and I will take your suggestions into account. I must be going, however. I'll pass on the hot chocolate this time."

"Huckleberry." For the first time, I heard an edge of steel in her voice. "I do want to help you, but that is only possible if you help me."

"As I said, I will think about what you've told me."

"I'm afraid I need a somewhat firmer commitment than that."

I shook my head in disbelief. "You want a firm commitment on who I choose to spend time with? Didn't you say that I'm effectively an adult and deserve to be treated like one?"

"Yes, of course," she protested. "But when your parents committed you to my care, I took on certain obligations to ensure your welfare."

"'Committed me to your care'," I resisted the temptation to mimic her voice, yet her words were ridiculous. "Your job is to run the camp that my parents are paying for and that's it." Again, I shook my head. "I tell you what, if I ever do become a psychologist, the first thing I'm going to do is be more honest with my patients than you are with your students."

A look of concern that seemed almost genuine crossed her forehead. "Huck, what is it you think we are doing here, you and me?"

The question was a stupid one, but it seemed rude to say that out loud. "I'm here for a 'holistic education'," I said wearily. "Oh, sure, I'm also meant to grow as a person, learn to be a contributing member of society and so on.

And, years from now, Warneford College will be in touch to ask for alumni donations. I know how it goes."

"Huck, what makes you think Warneford is a college?"

"Oh fine, hall of residence or whatever you call it. I never seem to get the Oxford terminology straight."

The look of concern was replaced by something else. Her face fought against her professional demeanour, eyebrows coming together and separating as if her forehead couldn't settle on an expression.

"I don't quite know how to say this, Huck. Though I believe that I owe you the truth. Do you think you are ready for that?"

This was becoming tedious. "Sure—hit me with the truth, Professor."

"Huck," she said slowly, "I am not your professor. I'm your therapist. And Warneford isn't a college or a hall of residence, it's a hospital. Yes, the Oxford Department of Experimental Psychology has offices here and runs this winter programme, but you are not a student in that programme—you are one of its patients."

I waited for the punchline. Professor Cholmondeley just stood there, her eyes searching mine; maybe she was waiting to see if I would laugh first.

OK fine, I'll blink, I thought. "Ha ha, very funny," I said.

Now she started to seem distressed. "Huck, please, I'm not trying to be funny."

"Congratulations, you're succeeding."

"When Mrs Sellwood first reached out to me about your case, I thought we might be able to help you. After what happened to her—"

"You mean after she was murdered by one of her patients," I interrupted, the words coming out before I realised my mouth was open.

"After the tragedy, your support network in New York was shattered. That's what we try to build up here at Warneford, an open community where high-functioning people suffering from a range of disorders can be helped and help each other so they can, eventually, live independently in society."

I had had enough of this. "I don't know why you're saying all this. So Kat, Mei, and Tshombe, they're all patients too?"

She said nothing, her face still struggling to control its expression. Then she nodded.

I played along with her story. "And what are they suffering from? Sure, Tshombe has a bunch of phobias and Mei is anxious all the time, but that's hardly a reason to lock someone up."

"Exactly." She was speaking carefully now, with the exaggerated calmness that always infuriated me. "This programme is not intended for people with severe disorders. Indeed, what our research group is most interested in is the borderline that defines normality."

A research group? This was a camp. Wasn't it? I looked at the wall on which a colourful poster advertised the Warneford Winter Programme. I had seen the poster before, but somehow the words seemed new. I unpinned it from the corkboard and held it in my hands.

"A holistic educational experience for exceptional teenagers," it read. "Teens from around the world come together in an experimental programme combining"—the words seemed to go in and out of focus of their own accord—"combining group therapy and individualised support to overcome mental and behavioural challenges. Led by experts from the Department of Experimental Psychology, the camp-like environment simulates an Oxford college to help all residents fulfil their potential." In cheery green, the final line read: "You are not your disorder."

The sound of my breathing was very loud. The noise of it was beginning to give me a headache. I needed fresh air, to breathe freely.

I needed to get out of there.

"Huck, I want you tell me what you understand of your surroundings," Professor Cholmondeley was saying. "Where are you, Huck?"

"I'm sorry, Professor—Dr Cholmondeley," I said, sticking the poster back on the wall. "I'm just a little tired and I was worried about my mother. Of course I understand where I am: the Warneford Winter Programme. My parents dropped me off here two and a half weeks ago. Group therapy and individualised support to overcome mental and behavioural challenges. Plus your suggestion about the Magna Carta and the benefit of seeing how writing can make things last was very helpful."

Her eyes narrowed. I couldn't be sure if she believed me. Was quoting the poster back at her too much? Regardless, I still needed to go.

"And we were wrong to sneak out earlier today," I added. "It won't happen again." It was only seven o'clock but I stifled a yawn. "Maybe we could keep talking about this tomorrow?" I offered.

She didn't seem convinced. "Very well, Huck," she said, stepping aside to let me pass. "If you're feeling tired, then we can pick this up again tomorrow." She took a look at her watch. "In any case, I must pay a visit to the infirmary. Apparently, Mr Farquhar contrived to slip on a banana peel after supper and has injured his back."

Couldn't happen to a nicer guy, I thought, taking a last look at the poster as I left. My face I kept neutral, imagining the placid expression of a compliant resident. I fingered the black wristband. Or an obedient prisoner.

I stepped in time with my heartbeat, struggling to keep both slow as I turned a corner away from Dr Cholmondeley. Why had my parents put me here? What the hell was wrong with me?

I had been seeing Mrs Sellwood for a long time, but she was more like a friend than a therapist. What did we talk about? I had it all written down in my diaries but those were at home in New York. It was something about writing. Something about the permanence of letters on the page.

Such were the thoughts going through my head as I neared my door. I was about to raise my wristband to unlock it when I saw that Tshombe's was ajar. Phobias or not, I generally felt good around him—so I knocked, then knocked again when there was no answer.

The door swung inward, blocked by something. "Tshombe?" I called. I leaned against the door and whatever the blockage was gave way, allowing me to enter the room.

The object blocking the door was Tshombe's foot. "Tshombe!" I cried, crouching down next to him. His shirt was covered in blood, glassy eyes staring up at the ceiling from where he lay. A surge of fear rose up inside me. I looked around the room but it was empty. I should help him, I should call for help, I knew. But as I reached to feel for a pulse I saw his lifeless throat covered in red and a wave of nausea swept over me.

Tears blinded me as I staggered to my feet, the hamburger from dinner sloshing about in my stomach. I looked for a trash can—rubbish bin—but Tshombe's room was neater than mine and it was nowhere to be found. He probably kept it in a closet. I was about to be sick, but I couldn't throw up on him.

I made it to the door and quickly swiped my own lock open. In my mind, I mapped out the steps to my own trash can, holding down the bile and half-digested food until I could grasp it in both hands. The door swung open and I lunged forward, but my mouth was already filling with acid and I vomited onto the carpet, reaching the metal tub only as the second wave of contractions purged my stomach of its contents. I knew I had to call for help, but as I took out my phone I saw the piece of paper I had stepped over when entering the room. It was another note constructed with letters clipped from newspapers, but this time the message was ominous:

Give Kat Hope
She deServes it

Fear yielded to panic. An image of Kat, also steeped in blood, came unbidden and caused me to retch once more, my empty gut collapsing in on itself. I forced myself up and out the door. I would phone for help, but if there was a chance of saving Kat I needed to act now.

I sprinted down the empty corridor to her room. Her door was shut, but when I hammered on it with my fist I thought I heard a muffled noise. I put my ear to the door and heard it again. There was no time. I stepped back across the hallway and charged the door with my shoulder. In a movie, it would have burst open, but I rebounded back and landed on the floor.

The window, I thought. I raced to the nearest exit leading to the courtyard and around to where her room opened onto it. The curtains were drawn, but the window was not locked. I hoisted the wooden frame up, dislodging a row of cigarette butts perched on the ledge. Lifting myself up, I swung my torso through the gap and was about to bring my legs through when I lost my grip on the frame. I clutched at the only thing I could reach, which was the curtain, and felt it tearing from the railings as I collapsed into the room.

Shaking the folds of material off me, I stood up to take in the room. On the chair by the desk, Kat sat bound and gagged. A rough rope wound around her body, lashing her to the chair. One of her own silk scarves had been forced between her teeth and tied behind her head. Her room was messier than Tshombe's, but whoever had done this to her had left.

Her eyes widened as I approached her and she struggled against the ropes. She tried to speak, but the scarf limited her to a frightened grunt. The rope looked painful, though she did not seem to be injured. At least there was no blood.

I stepped behind her and undid the knot holding the scarf, which she spat out onto the floor.

"Who did this to you?" I cried. "Where is he?"

She looked at me with a mix of fear and anger. "What are you talking about?"

"Tshombe—" I began. "We have to get help."

"Huck, what happened to Tshombe?"

"He was hurt, like Mrs Sellwood," I spoke haltingly. "There was blood, so much blood." The thought nearly made me retch again. "But then I saw the note," I said.

"What note?"

"I saw the note," I said more confidently, "and so I came to save you."

"Save me?" Now there was contempt in her voice as well as fear. "Save me from whom?"

I shook my head, as her responses made no sense. "I came to save you from whoever did this to you, whoever stabbed Tshombe."

Now she looked at me in disbelief. "Huck," she said

slowly. "*You're* the one who tied me up here." Her eyes moved down to look at my hands.

There was blood on her face where the gag had been. And blood on the curtains that I had climbed through.

"And *you're* the one holding a knife," she continued.

I followed her gaze down to see that my hands, dripping and red, still gripped the hunting knife.

"Oh my God, Huck," Kat whispered. "What have you done?"

And from fingers still wet with Tshombe's blood, the blade slipped out and clattered to the ground.

Part Three

Now

"Come down from the ledge, Huck."

A new voice, speaking calmly, reaches out to the better angels of my nature. But first you have to battle the demons.

"No," I say. "I see it all so clearly now. This is how it ends. This is how the killing ends. You will all be safe after I'm gone."

"You haven't hurt anyone, Huck—yet. The only person at risk here is you."

I shake my head. "His blood is all over me." In the moonlight, the blood is a black stain on my hand. "The other stabbings. Mrs Sellwood. Maybe that was me also."

"Tshombe's alive, Huck. He's down there, waiting for you."

It is so tempting, to believe, that I almost do. Looking over the edge, the courtyard is shrouded in darkness. There is movement, but that could be anyone.

"It's better this way," I say, preparing myself. "Neater. No explanations, no notes. Just darkness."

"Wait, Huck." The voice is pleading now, edging closer. "I've been where you are now. You may not believe me now, but what you're feeling is temporary. It gets better. You aren't alone, Huck."

I look over the edge once more.

The new voice presses on. "Can't you see that this is what she wants you to do? She's tricking you. She fooled us all."

An echo of a memory makes me pause. A missing piece of a different story. "What happened to the knife?" I ask.

"What knife?"

"She was holding the knife. I heard it scraping against the stone."

A different kind of concern enters the new voice. "She's up here? Huck, she is the one who is dangerous. Where is she?"

The rain gathering on my cheeks feels like water, the moisture on my hand feels like blood, but how could I be sure. "Is this real?" I ask the night.

The new footsteps have gone quiet. Maybe the new voice is hunting the old voice. I should really get on, but now I'm curious which one will prevail. The dampness on my face runs down to my mouth in a tiny rivulet. It tastes salty—tears, then. I wipe my eyes; without thinking, I use the hand still holding the parchment. Funny, as I hold it up in the moonlight there are faint lines running beneath the words, keeping the writing in order.

Poor Mrs Sellwood. She would have told me to set aside time to mourn. That it's OK to grieve, to cry. Instead, I squashed those feelings into a ginger beer bottle and corked it, put it up high on a shelf and waited for it to explode.

I'm sorry, Mrs Sellwood. I don't know how I lost track.

After you died, everything overwhelmed me. Mom and Dad did their best, but I know they found it hard. A change is as good as a holiday, Mom said. So, they shipped me off here to start again. It's what you had wanted for me, they said. I'd always been good at tests and interviews; getting into the programme was easy. Keeping track of what's real and what's not, though—that's no piece of cake.

And so now we have to go back to the beginning again. Go over it with care, Huck, like Mrs Sellwood used to tell me. If you keep a diary, you can keep track of what is real and what is not. One diary for your dreams, the other for real life. Fiction and non-fiction sections in the library. Just be sure that you keep the two books separate, or you don't know what might happen.

Consciousness is a story that we tell ourselves. But what if that story is a lie?

Then

13

Who, exactly, is a diary written for? I never understood people who publish their diaries, let alone the people who buy them. Could there be anything more pretentious than selling your musings, scribbled at the end of the day, organised only by the humdrum chronology of your march toward death?

History will be kind to me, Winston Churchill is thought to have said, for I intend to write it. He, however, knew how to edit and how to embellish. He certainly knew better than to share the raw work-in-progress that is daily existence.

If a newspaper is history's first draft, a diary is the roughest sketch of a self-portrait—the outlines of a cheekbone, the angle of a nose. No fool would share that sketch with the world; nor would he miss the opportunity to improve it a little, make the cheekbone a touch more angular, the nose a tad more graceful.

The difference is that a diary is episodic. You don't come back to the same sketch, you may not even be using the same pen and paper. And though a sketch of a person must normally have a head, two eyes, a nose, and so on, the choice of what to include or exclude in a diary is more complicated. Sometimes you have to read between the lines; sometimes you have to read between the pages.

Back in Kat's room, I stared at my fingers and the knife that lay next to my foot, a small circle of red seeping from its blade into the carpet. Stepping toward Kat, I saw her flinch.

"I won't hurt you," I said.

"You've told me that before," she replied as I knelt beside her to untie the rope.

It was a complicated and messy knot. "You say I did this to you?"

"At first, I thought it was a bit of role play—you know, something a little kinky. But the knots got tighter and then you walked out the door. You really don't remember?"

I shook my head. "None of this makes any sense." Finally, I managed to get an end of the rope clear and Kat could wriggle free. When she did, she backed away from me, looking at my hands. I looked down also; they were still red with blood. Tshombe's blood.

"We have to get to Tshombe," I blurted out. "I found him and then saw the note about you. I was about to call for help." Explanations could wait. I opened the door and ran down the corridor. After a moment's hesitation, I heard Kat following behind me.

As we approached Tshombe's door, I slowed. It was still ajar. I nudged it, not wanting to hit his leg again, but this time it swung wide open. The room was empty.

"He was right here," I said, confused. "How can I remember seeing him here, dying or dead, and not remember tying you up?"

Kat's fear of me seemed to be subsiding. She put a tentative hand on my arm. "It was you, but it wasn't you," she said. "You were in some kind of daze. You kept mumbling about a Mrs Sellwood and that you needed to finish what you had started—that it would all be over soon. That with her out of the way, you could finally be free. What did you mean?"

What had I meant? What had I done? "I'm so sorry," I said. "I don't recall any of that." I couldn't possibly have hurt Mrs Sellwood. An hour ago I would have said the same thing about hurting Kat or Tshombe.

"The whole time," she continued, "you didn't look me in the eye. Did you sleepwalk as a kid?"

"Not that I know of," I replied, still looking for signs of what had happened. I kneeled down to look at the floor. Dark spots dotted the carpet, but I couldn't tell if they were old or new.

"And you don't remember what happened to Tshombe either?"

"No," I said. "I mean I don't *know* what happened to Tshombe before I found him."

"It's OK." She rubbed my arm. "We'll get through this together."

"But I don't understand—where's Tshombe?"

"Is it possible that you imagined seeing him?"

I held out my bloodstained hands. "Look at my hands, are you imagining that also?" A thought occurred to me and I took out my phone, calling Tshombe's number. A polite English voice announced that his device was off or out of range.

"Maybe he got up and walked away?" Kat asked helplessly.

"I can't see how he could have walked anywhere."

"Then someone must have moved his body."

I scratched my head. "Who would do such a thing? Why?"

"I don't know," she said. "But I've never trusted Cholmondeley. What if she decided that a dead student was a threat to Warneford? Or that police attention might reveal what she's been up to in the clock tower?"

My head was beginning to swim. I knew I should be worried about Tshombe, or grieving for him, but first I needed to get my head straight.

"I need some time to think," I said, leaning against the wall next to my door. "Kat, I can't begin to apologise for scaring you like that. Can you ever forgive me?" I reached out to hold her, but once more she flinched.

Then she relented and took my hand in hers. "OK," she said. "You get your head together and I'll go and see what I can find out about Tshombe. I'll call you if I learn anything." She started down the corridor before stopping in her tracks. "Oh, I almost forgot," she added. "Oliver—the porter—let me borrow the key to the tower for the night. I say 'borrow', though he would probably say 'steal'. As long as I get it back to his office before dawn, it's pretty much the same thing."

As she walked away, I held up my wristband to the door and opened it. The smell of vomit hit me immediately, almost causing me to retch anew. Despite the cold night air, I opened the window as wide as it would go and used half a box of tissues to clean up the floor as best I could. Tying the plastic bag that lined my bin with a double knot, the stench began to abate. I washed my hands in the small basin and sat at my desk, stealing some stillness and silence.

The last of the four mysterious notes I had received lay next to my lamp. I took out the other three and looked at them together. Some of the letters were clearly from a single publication. I couldn't be sure, but they looked like they had been cut by the same hand. The paper on which they had been stuck was nothing special, the type used in the college photocopiers and printers. I had a stack of it in a desk drawer myself.

As the turmoil in my head began to settle, I tried to make sense of what I knew, and what I knew I didn't know. The problem, of course, was that which I didn't know I didn't know.

Set it down on paper, Mrs Sellwood used to say. A problem shared is a problem halved, even if you're only sharing it with your diary. Be assured that your future self, reading it, will have made it past whatever crisis confronts you now. A diary entry isn't some message stuck in a bottle and cast into the sea. A diary entry is a time capsule, in stasis until at some appointed time it is opened and revealed to the world.

But what if it is never read, or read by the wrong person? I had asked at the time. Well then, she replied, in the former case it means that the appointed time has not yet arrived. That doesn't mean it never will. And in the latter case, if someone else reads your diary, they can hardly travel back in time and hurt the previous you, now can they? In the end, everything will be OK. And if it is not OK, then it is not yet the end.

I smiled at the memory of Mrs Sellwood. I should be grieving for her too, I knew. Yet until I started thinking more clearly, I wasn't much use to anyone.

I reached into my backpack for the leather-bound journal Mom had given me, but my hand came out empty. I opened the zip and looked inside, then around the room. The muscles in my neck began to tense and I felt another wellspring of panic.

In my entire life, I had only ever lost one of my eighty-seven journals. It happened when I was fourteen and I left it on the breakfast table. After an hour of searching, we worked out that Dad must have folded it up into a pile of newspapers that went out for recycling. That morning he had just made it in time for the truck, which trundled off with the waste paper. Phone calls to the company went unanswered so I got my pocket money and took the subway and a ferry to the paper mill in Staten Island. I spent most of the day wandering through piles of waste before admitting defeat. I returned home after dark, locking myself in my room as I tried to recreate six weeks of memories. From then on, my diaries were only ever in my room, my backpack, or my hands.

The journal was not in my hands or my backpack, but it was conceivable that I had placed it elsewhere in my room. Starting with the desk, I went through the drawers, then the bookshelf and under my bed. For completeness I looked in the closet as well, careful not to disturb the newspaper in which the burned Magna Carta lay. The other shelves had shirts and trousers folded neatly and not so neatly, but nothing seemed to have been disturbed.

Moving more quickly, I pulled clothes out of the closet, at first laying and then throwing them onto my bed. There was no sign of the diary, but as I reached the top shelf and took out an oversize woollen sweater, it revealed an ice cream container of some English brand that I had not seen before.

The container was light; it looked to have been cleaned and reused as a kind of Tupperware. I set it down on the desk and prised off the top to look inside. My fingers felt numb as they ran through the contents before I tipped them onto the desk. A well-used glue stick hit the surface first, followed by a snowfall of paper cut into small pieces. Scattering across the desk, the smallest tumbled in time with my breath. Some were an inch square, others a quarter of that, each piece a letter cut from a newspaper that I now recognised as the *New York Post*, ready to be used in a ransom note from a previous century—or an untraceable warning to an Oxford student in this one.

14

There was a loud knock on the door.

"Huck?" It was Dr Cholmondeley, knocking with the same silver ring she used to get attention in the dining hall.

"Just a minute," I called out, scooping the loose letters off the desk and back into the ice cream container. The four completed notes I folded and put in my pocket. Stains of vomit were still visible on the carpet; there was nothing I could do about that now.

I opened the door. Dr Cholmondeley stood in the hallway, arms folded. She looked past me to the open window then sniffed at the air, now resembling a bloodhound more than a duck. "Are you sure everything is OK, Huck?"

Tshombe could be dead, Kat had been bound and gagged—by me, it seemed—no, everything was far from OK.

"Sure," I said. I put a hand to my stomach and nodded over my shoulder. "I think I might have been a little too enthusiastic about hamburger night."

Her nose twitched, but she carried on. "I wanted to apologise," she said, "for how our earlier conversation went. Would you come with me to my office? You're welcome to another hot chocolate—if your stomach is up to it."

That was the last thing I wanted to do, but didn't have the strength to refuse. The corridors passed in a blur as we moved down them once more.

"I didn't mean to drive you away," she said, "but you caught me by surprise. You had appeared to be settling in so well. I thought we were making real progress."

The joke—it was a joke, wasn't it?—hadn't gotten any funnier. The pressure inside my head was increasing. "Progress toward what?"

"Huck—" She turned the ring on her finger. "You have a clear idea why you are here at Warneford, what your parents sent you here for, correct?"

No, I thought. "Sure," I said again.

"But you do sometimes have problems with your memory, remembering things?"

Why I was here, where my diary was, what the hell had happened to Tshombe and Kat. "Mark Twain once said that if you tell the truth, you don't have to remember anything," I said. "Mom wrote that down for me once, but I could never find the original quote." Professor Cholmondeley was still looking at me. "OK, occasionally I forget stuff," I conceded. "Though I might not remember that, right?"

"Good, good." She smiled. "Yes, it's a particular challenge when a symptom masks its own diagnosis. But that's one of the things we have been working on together."

We had reached the door of her office, which she held open for me.

"Working on how?"

She pointed me toward a chair as she sat behind the desk. "Talking about our memories, strategies for organising information. It's entirely possible that you have forgotten these sessions also."

"You're saying that I have some kind of amnesia?" I wasn't a homeless guy walking around having forgotten his own name. I knew who I was. At least, I thought I did. In my pocket, my phone began to ring. Mom. Not now—I dismissed the call.

"We tend to avoid labels here," Professor Cholmondeley said.

"Yeah, I get it," I said. "'You are not your disorder.'"

"Ah yes, you remember that from the brochure. The written word seems to have a special role for you, doesn't it? Memory loss is a difficult burden to bear and can make many ordinary tasks more challenging. Later in life, it can make it hard to hold down a job or a steady relationship. Mrs Sellwood had been working with you on techniques to deal with those challenges."

Mrs Sellwood. My diaries. Gaps that I couldn't explain. My phone pinged—a message from Mom. I switched it to silent. Without thinking, my hand reached up to feel the scar at my hairline near the temple. A cut like that must have required stitches. Lots of stitches. How could I not remember that?

"Did I hit my head?" I whispered.

Dr Cholmondeley nodded. "Some years ago, you were

in an accident. A car crash. You and your father were lucky to survive. But yes, you suffered a head injury and that affected the way your brain stores memories."

"My father was driving?" The photo of him and Mom in a convertible, years before I was born, was the only memory I had of him driving a car. Was this the thing for which I was meant to forgive him? "Why don't I remember the crash?"

"Sometimes you do," she said. "It seems to help if you write things down. This is now the fifth time we are having a variation of this conversation. You said you had misplaced your diary, which is why you are now writing down notes on Warneford letterhead."

I looked down at the notepad in my hands, the black scrawl of my handwriting snaking across the page. At the bottom was a single word with a question mark. "Kat?"

"And what about Kat," I asked. "What's her problem?"

"That is what I had wanted to warn you about," Dr Cholmondeley said. "Most of our residents are not a danger to themselves or anyone else." Again, she played with the band of silver on her index finger. "And we do not generally discuss medical histories or other personal matters with residents or anyone else. But Miss Evershaw has a history of—of antisocial behaviour, a lack of empathy and remorse. I thought we had been making progress. Such cases are notoriously difficult to treat, however, and I now believe that much of her progress was faked—that she has been hiding the full extent of her condition."

I recognised this description. "You're saying she's a psychopath?"

"Once again, that is your term, not mine."

"Kat isn't a psychopath. She's angry; she's a teenager. It sounds like she's got a right to be angry at the world after what she's been through."

Dr Cholmondeley nodded again. "There may be some truth to that. Nonetheless, she has the potential to harm other people. To harm you, Huck."

If only she knew—Kat was the one in danger. But there was more going on here. "Why are you trying to keep us apart?"

"As I said earlier, my only concern is your welfare. I am not opposed to you forming relationships, even close ones. But this obsession with the tower has to stop."

And then I saw it, written in my own hand on the Warneford notepaper. The single word, "tower", circled and underlined. All of this—her vendetta against Kat, confusing me about my memories—all of this was to prevent me going with Kat into the tower to discover its secrets. Kat had the key. If we could get inside once more, all of this would start to make sense. First I had to get out of Cholmondeley's office, but I was done being diplomatic.

"You know what *I* think?" I said. "I think it's *you* that's crazy. Either this is a sick practical joke you're playing—there are hidden cameras and I'm getting punk'd, or something. Or else you've lost your mind. What I do know is that I don't have to sit here and listen to any more of your garbage."

"Huck, please don't make this harder than it has to be."

"Or what? Or you'll throw me in some rubber room you've got hidden under the college? You know what, I *was* crazy. I was crazy to listen to you and your lies. And that's the real truth. Even you don't believe what you're saying. It's all just a way of trying to keep me away from the tower—and what lies beneath it."

I smiled as the look of alarm returned to her face. "Oh yes, we know all about the little secret that you and Sir Michael have been keeping."

"Whatever Kat has told you about the tower—it is something that she has invented on her own. I don't know why she would do this, but I'm trying to warn you that you are in danger." Once more, she spoke in that infuriatingly calm voice. "Huck, I think you are getting distressed. Allow me to call one of the orderlies to help you back to your room."

Her hand moved to the edge of the desk and she pressed something beneath it. There was no sound, but I had seen enough movies about bank robberies to know what a silent alarm was. I had no desire to find out who would respond to it.

"Apologies, doc," I said. "But I must be off." I stood and made for the door. She called out something as I opened it, though I was beyond listening. I started to head to my room, though if a security team really did respond to her call then that was the first place they would go. So I turned and ran to the nearest exit, which led out to the courtyard.

It was beginning to rain again, a mist falling in the darkness. I wore only a light sweater that was already beading with droplets. A pain behind my eyes was starting to spread, the kind of headache I had not experienced for years.

What she said made no sense. I was not a patient. Sure, I had some issues but everyone has issues. And if I wasn't a student why was I taking all these classes and tests? OK, so maybe a lot of those tests seemed to focus on my feelings and my memories, which would be hard to grade on a curve. But, but, but.

Across the courtyard stood the clock tower. Light came from the doorway at its base, which was ajar. Let's solve one mystery at a time, I thought, and ran toward it.

15

The tower loomed over me as I approached. From outside Warneford's walls, I could hear the Christmas carollers still braving the cold. My walk in the meadow with Kat earlier that evening, when we first heard them burst into song, felt like days ago.

Of course, Warneford was a college. Why she would want to play such a trick on a student—pretending that it was not—was beyond me. So what if Mei cut herself, or Tshombe's dad talked about sending him here to cure him of his fears. That proved nothing. Teenagers have all sorts of angst. Perhaps April Fool's Day was celebrated at Christmastime in England. Or perhaps Cholmondeley was willing to do anything to keep us from learning the truth about the tower. Could that include killing Tshombe and hiding his body?

I shivered as I reached the heavy door that led into the base of the tower. The prospect of protection from the drizzle was inviting, but I wanted to know what I would be walking into. The lock on the door hung loose, the door itself was open a few inches. I peered inside.

New temporary lights dangled from hooks driven into the stone walls, illuminating the floor and casting odd shadows up the stairs and into the blackness above. Extension cords snaked down to a generator humming away in the corner, next to the gardening equipment and paint cans that I had seen on my last visit. At the threshold, where I stood, the stone flooring was scored with the traffic of machinery that had come and gone since then. The focus of that attention was now clear: a hole in the floor beneath the tower, at least six feet across. Planks had been laid down around it marking a rough square, covering jagged edges of rock. A low barrier was erected on top of the planks, reminiscent of a child's playpen made of rusting steel pipes.

I nudged the door open and stepped inside. It was a relief to be out of the rain, though the chamber was now infused with a musty smell. At first, I thought it was simply moisture coming from outside, but then I saw what filled the hole at the base of the tower. Freshly poured concrete rose to six inches below the planks, steel reinforcement bars sticking out of the top. The smooth concrete contrasted with the roughly hewn stone that made up the rest of the tower. I walked up to the low barrier and dropped a small rock onto the concrete, which was quite dry.

"Whatever was there is gone now." The voice belonged to Kat, who was descending the stairs. She must have been watching me from the shadows when I entered. I now saw that her shoulder bag was on the ground among the paint cans.

"Why fill it with concrete?" I asked.

"Maybe this way, no one will ever be able to see what was down there."

I ran my hand along the barrier. "Or maybe they really are shoring up the foundations of this old tower."

Kat, still wary of me, hesitated on the last step.

"Any news about Tshombe?" I asked.

She shook her head.

"I should tell you, Cholmondeley specifically warned me to stay away from here—and from you."

"Oh? Did she say why?"

"I think it was partly to keep us from finding out what has been going on here."

"I've been trying to figure that out myself," she replied. "My best guess is that a frame was set up above the hole. You can see indentations in the floor outside the planks. Then a pulley system was used to lift something out."

"Something heavy?"

"Look at the indentations."

The stones that lined the floor had square marks about the size of my hand. I had no way to measure the load, but to leave such indentations it must have been big. "Then what—logs greased with animal fat?"

She laughed—a good sign that she might yet trust me once again. "Either that or Merlin and his giant helped move it out. In any case, the door is wide enough."

I tried to imagine manoeuvring one of the massive slabs of rock from Stonehenge within this space. "Or else they smashed it and took only the sword," I mused.

Kat walked down the final step and moved toward me. "I suppose it depends on your view of the legend, and whether you think that only the true king—or queen—could pull out the sword." She stopped just beyond arm's reach. "So, how are you feeling?"

My head was aching, but that was a distraction. Kat's bag was still on the ground by the paint cans so I moved to get it for her. "OK, I guess. Confused. I'm so sorry about what happened earlier. And Cholmondeley was acting very strange. She was trying to convince me that Warneford isn't a college or a hall of residence but a hospital."

"Really? Why do you think she would say such a thing?" Kat followed me toward the cans.

"I don't know. She never struck me as much of a practical joker. But why else would she do it?" I leaned down to pick up Kat's bag, which was resting against one of the tins.

"Who knows?" she said, now next to me.

As I lifted the bag, I noticed that the tin it was leaning against wasn't paint at all. "Potassium nitrate," I read the label aloud. "That rings a bell."

"It should," said Kat, reaching for her bag. "It's saltpetre—the stuff that burned out the message on our Magna Carta. I found it down here. Kind of amazing that people are using the same thing centuries later—though today it's used mainly for removing tree stumps."

I nodded. The tin was sealed tight, so it was probably my imagination, but I thought that I could once again smell the burning parchment. The memory of Kat igniting it sent a shudder through me. I passed her the bag, the bag in which she had stolen the Magna Carta from the museum—though, when it came to evidence of our crime, the half-destroyed vellum in my closet was still Exhibit A.

As she swung the bag onto her shoulder in a practised move, the flap lifted up. In the flickering light, I could have sworn that a green corner poked out—the green corner of a leather-bound journal. Without thinking, I grabbed the bag in mid-air. I had a handful of the flap, the bag itself suspended between us with the contents on display. And sitting in the middle, next to cigarette packets, some yellowed papers, and her phone, was my diary.

"What the hell?" I exclaimed.

Her eyes followed mine to the journal. She sighed. "I'm so sorry, Huck. I didn't mean to steal it. I wanted to borrow it for a while. I took it from your backpack and was going to slip it back in tonight before—before everything went so crazy."

"Borrow it? Why?"

"I know, it's a terrible thing to do." She shook her head. "It sounds stupid, but I thought it might help me to understand you better. When you told me about that dream you had—the one in which your spirit occupied the body of a woman—it completely freaked me out. I've never shared something like that with anyone in my life. It excited me, but it also scared me."

"So you stole my diary?"

"*Borrowed,*" she repeated. "I thought if I could see a little more of what's in your head, I would know whether I could trust you. I'm sorry, I know it must feel like a terrible violation." She rubbed her arm where the rope had bound her earlier in the evening. "Though, to be honest, you haven't exactly been a profile in good manners this evening yourself."

The bag swung between us. I was so relieved at finding the journal that I was ready to forgive her there and then. "And did you?" I asked.

"What?"

"Understand me better?"

Kat took another step toward me, lowering the bag as she did. She reached out to my cheek, the first time she had touched me since I untied her. "A little," she said with a sly grin.

She was close enough that I could smell the last cigarette on her breath, mixed with traces of perfume from her neck. I let go of the bag, which landed softly on the ground, tumbling onto its side as I wrapped my arms around her. The green of her eyes was the same shade as the leather of my diary; gold flecks echoing the yellow of the paper that had now fallen out of her bag and onto the floor.

Her red lips were inches from my own. "Do you promise not to tie me up again?" she whispered.

I laughed, looking down as I did. "I prom—" I began, and stopped as I saw that the yellow paper that had slid from her shoulder bag onto the floor next to my diary was not paper at all.

It was vellum.

I released Kat and crouched down to pick up the folded piece of parchment. Opening it, the familiar cramped text of the medieval scribe spread out before me. "*Johannes Dei gracia...*" It was the Magna Carta, intact and undamaged, as real as the one that I had seen in my room, the one that Kat had set fire to. I rubbed it between my fingers; it had the same fragile texture, it even smelled the same. But who knew what eight-hundred-year-old calfskin smelled like? The edges were frayed, the text was patchy, exactly as we had seen in the Ashmolean. Yet as I held it up to the light and turned it over, the reverse side showed the only imperfection, a single line of text in modern typography: "© Salisbury Cathedral, MMXV." The mark of the Cathedral's copyright, dated 2015, presumably for Magna Carta's—the real Magna Carta's—800th anniversary.

"What—" My voice sounded hollow, like a stranger in another room. "What is this?" I was still crouched by her bag. The cigarette lighter had tumbled out, and my fingers trembled as I picked that up as well.

"Oh, come now, Huck. I would have thought you'd recognise the Magna Carta when you see it?" She picked up the bag, slipping my diary back inside, and fished around for a cigarette.

"Give me a light, would you?"

I put the lighter in my pocket, holding the parchment in both hands. "The parchment in my room, the one we burned, it's the same as this? A copy?"

"Well, if you're going to be pedantic about it, they're all copies," she said easily, replacing the cigarette in the packet. "Scribes were more common than photocopiers back in the thirteenth century. Though yes, the parchment in your room is similar to this. I bought a couple, as I couldn't rely on getting it right the first time. Have you ever tried to write with a saltpetre paste? It's a nightmare! Trying to keep the letters clear enough to read, using just enough so that you can see the message without the whole thing going up in smoke. So I bought a few copies to practise on. This was an extra—I probably should have disposed of it earlier."

"You bought copies—from the gift store?"

"Yes. Actually, it was Tshombe who gave me the idea." She looked at me. "Oh, I see you are upset. To be honest, I was terribly flattered that you believed I could have stolen a priceless artefact on a whim."

"But you made it all up? Excalibur? Stonehenge? Why would you do such a thing?"

"I didn't make up anything that you didn't want to believe. Listen to yourself." She took my diary and flicked to an early page. "*As a kid, I loved stories about medieval England—King Arthur and the rest of it. I wrote one in which a young boy from New York is the only person who can pull Excalibur from its stone. He goes on to become a wise and beloved ruler. It was so much simpler than succeeding in real life.*"

I felt the room begin to spin and leaned against the barrier by the hole. Released from my grip, the counterfeit vellum floated to the floor. "But we went to Stonehenge—we met that guy, Arthur Uther Pendragon. Was he some actor that you hired to play along?"

"Arthur?" She smiled at this. "No, he's real enough. But he's also an alcoholic. If you promise him a few cans of lager, he's up for anything. I called to say we were on a scavenger hunt and that he was one of the clues. He seemed happy enough to play along."

"This was a game for you?"

The room was becoming stuffy and I was having trouble breathing.

"We all have our weaknesses, Huckleberry." A coldness

had entered her voice, or perhaps it was that the warmth had left it. "Mine is games. Life is so deathly dull otherwise. Earn money, have a family, live till you're a hundred. Yawn. No wonder our generation spends half our time online. The problem is that online, the stakes are so petty. How many followers, how many likes. I prefer my games to have consequences."

"What, what are you talking about?" I sputtered.

"I'm talking about you going to prison for the murder of poor, dear Tshombe. You did, after all, confess to me and your fingerprints are all over the murder weapon."

"The body—" I began. "There's no body."

"A temporary problem. You're probably right that Cholmondeley moved it to avoid scandal. Now that I've called the police, however, the sniffer dogs will find it in a jiffy. They're rather good at that sort of thing. Plus"—she turned to a more recent page in the diary—"we have here a confession of sorts: *I followed her gaze down to see that my hands, dripping and red, still gripped the hunting knife. 'Oh my God, Huck,' Kat whispered. 'What have you done?' And from fingers still wet with Tshombe's blood, the blade slipped out and clattered to the ground.* Sound familiar? Sometimes, the things dearest to us are the ones we hurt the most. Is that why you killed this Mrs Sellwood you keep talking about?"

The spinning of the room accelerated and I had to brace myself to stay upright. None of this made sense. The words were mine and yet not mine, memories and yet not memories. I needed to focus and the one certainty was that I had to get my diary back. And then I had to get away.

Kat was browsing through it still, looking for another

passage to read. Pushing myself off the safety rail, I lurched toward her, grabbing at the leather cover. She twisted away from me and the diary fanned open. Instead of the cover, I got hold of a few pages, the stitching holding tight as we fought over it. Then I felt a stabbing pain in my shin as she kicked me with her heavy shoes. Still I held onto the pages, but a new sound cut through the still air of the room, the shriek of tearing paper.

I felt it like a physical blow, a single page coming loose into my hand as I fell to the floor. The only words I could make out were scrawled in large letters: *Caliburnus in stanengem abscondetur.*

In a daze, I picked myself up. Kat now held a knife, the knife I had dropped in her room—or the knife she told me I had dropped in her room. "Stay back, Huck," she said. "I'd hate to have to hurt you."

If I couldn't get the diary, I still had to get out, to clear my head. She was between me and the door, but I could make it to the stairs. At least to breathe fresh air, to think. My plan went no further than that, but it was better than no plan at all.

As I started up the stairs, her laughter followed me. "Oh Huckleberry, you're so predictable! *The banister is slick and aids neither balance nor grip. I reach another wooden landing and pause to catch my breath, panting clouds of vapour into the cold night air. The wood creaks under my weight—too many kebabs, I guess.* You've already written this, and I've already read it, Huck," she called after me. "We both know how it ends."

We both know how it ends.

16

A French literary theorist once published a manifesto called "The Death of the Author". Authors don't control the meaning of their words, he argued. Pretending that they did was to confuse interpretation with biography. An author's experiences, his or her preferences and prejudices, shouldn't be the basis for interpreting text. Such an approach imposed an artificial order, a certainty, on the meaning of that text, fixing it in time and space. Meaning, he argued, was to be found not at the source—the act of writing—but at its destination—the act of reading.

Discovering this as a teenager was incredibly liberating. Don't foist your meaning on me, Mr Shakespeare—*I* will tell you what Hamlet means when he says, "To be, or not to be: that is the question." Yet liberation was followed by dislocation. If I could do that to Shakespeare, anyone else could do it to my words. In the slippery post-modern world, how could I be sure what I meant?

Unless I kept those words for myself. How did the

argument apply to a text that was never intended to be read by anyone else? If there was no reader and the author was dead, did the text die also?

Such thoughts rose, unbidden, as I raced up the steps in search of air, in search of clarity. I heard Kat chasing after me, heavy shoes clattering on the stairs. I gripped the fragment of text, its Latin incantation beginning to bleed ink down the page.

Poor Mrs Sellwood. I had no memory of our last meeting beyond the argument. I couldn't have killed her. You don't get to walk away from a thing like that. There are consequences. Jail time. Juvenile detention, at least.

Unless you're insane.

My legs kept moving. The pain in the left one was becoming unbearable, aching like the scar on my temple, a jackhammer pounding into my brain.

When I reached the balcony I paused, a moment of beauty before the end. A dramatic end to the tale about to begin.

And then I saw that the true end was indeed the death of the author. An end to sorrow and confusion, to suffering and embarrassment. The serpent in my ear told me to jump and I climbed onto the ledge.

But there was an interruption, another voice, another story to be told.

And everything before the "but" was a lie.

Now

"Mei?" I call out to the new voice. "Is that you?"

There is no answer. I step down from the ledge onto the balcony. My clothes are soaked and I start to shiver as I follow the balcony back toward the archway, feeling my way to avoid tripping in the dark.

In the dim light at the top of the stairwell, I see Mei's outline. She must have retreated there after I told her Kat was here also. A finger to her lips urges me to keep quiet.

"What about your parents?" I whisper. "You were about to fly home."

"A trick," she says under her breath. "Someone claiming to be from the Embassy said they were arranging a ticket—that seemed suspicious from the outset. But I was worried about my parents and didn't want to miss the flight. Only when I was in the car to the airport did I manage to reach my uncle, who then put my parents themselves on the line. Mainly, they were disappointed that I'd been fooled so easily."

She peers around the side of the archway. Still no sign of Kat. "I made the car turn around. Then I caught up with

Tshombe, who told me what she had asked him to do."

"Tshombe's OK?" I say. My voice sounds hoarse.

"He's fine," she replies. "Fake blood and the death scene in *Hamlet.* Kat said it would be hilarious to trick you into thinking that Jack the Ripper had snuck in and killed him." She wiped the drizzle from her glasses. "OK, in retrospect, none of that sounds like a good idea. Anyway, I went to Dr Cholmondeley. She said you two had an argument and that you were going on about the tower and that she was worried. Later, when I saw the door open downstairs—" She stops speaking, finger now on my own lips to prevent me starting.

I look also, but there is no movement outside.

"You don't understand," I speak as quietly as I can. "She's got my diary."

"And?" Mei mimes.

"The diary helps me keep track of what's real—and what's not," I try to explain. "And she seems to think that the end of this story has already been written."

"So, write a different ending." Even in a whisper, the exasperation in Mei's voice is clear.

"But then it wouldn't be a tragedy," Kat says, turning the corner of the balcony and approaching the archway. "And happy endings are so *boring.*" In her hand, reflections in the blade of the knife are the only source of light on the tower. Her other hand holds my diary. "Now, Huckleberry, patience isn't one of my virtues. Are you going to be a good boy and jump? Don't tell me you're having second thoughts. Chester had second thoughts also, but"—she eyes the blade in her hand—"I can be persuasive."

The prospect of a knife wound worries me less than the need to understand what Kat has done to me. "You said there were two bodies, a boy and a girl. Yet it was only Chester who died that day."

A look of confusion crosses her brow. "Part of me died that day also. I loved Chester." The confusion clears. "But then life goes on."

"Did you burn a Magna Carta for him also?" I counter. "Lure him in with tales of Excalibur?"

"Oh, heavens no, that was just for you, darling," she replies sweetly. And then the warmth vanishes. "Chester was more of a Holy Grail man. Fortunately, the Templars are very versatile when it comes to conspiracy theories. I believe Mei made that very same point quite recently, didn't you Mei?"

Mei begins to take a step forward but I put an arm out to stop her. "Stay behind me," I urge with a voice braver than I feel.

"Are you kidding?" She kindly but firmly pushes me to the side. "My parents forced me to do six years of competitive taekwondo. No insult intended, but I'm not sure you could fight your way out of a paper bag."

"Oh, really?" Kat sounds unimpressed. "*I* had to survive Friday nights at the Basingstoke Arms with my modesty intact. Don't worry, though, I'll be kind to your memories. I'll say that the two of us rushed up here to stop Huck from jumping—and that Mei heroically tried to grab his hand as he did, only to plummet with him down onto the courtyard below." She wipes an imaginary tear from her eye. "It will be very sad."

"Somehow, I don't think that's going to happen," Mei counters, edging forward, fists raised.

I can't let Mei fight her alone and the balcony is too narrow to stand side by side. I follow the narrow path the long way around the tower, aiming to get behind Kat and flank her. Turning the last corner, I arrive in time to see Mei aim a kick at Kat's knife hand, knocking it against the wall. Kat must have been charging Mei, as she crashes into her, causing them both to fall to the ground.

The knife and the diary land on the stone. Kat quickly regains her footing, recovering the blade. She stands in the archway, panting in the cold night air. "I'm afraid there's no way out but down. You can hold hands if you like. We could add a whole star-crossed-lovers element." She dries the knife on her dress.

In my hand, the page of my diary is soaked and has started to tear. It seems ludicrous to carry it into a fight, so I start to lay it down on the ledge.

"Oh, you and your precious diary," Kat calls out to me. "You do know it's the diary that sealed your fate. I'll be sure to publish it, by the way. Years from now, people will study it, trying to get inside the head of the boy who thought he could find Excalibur—before that same head was crushed against Warneford's cobblestones. The boy who confessed to murdering his friend because I told him that he'd done it. You're not much of a writer, though—you make us all sound like old farts. No, correction: you make us all sound like *you.* But in any case, you'll be famous! You should thank me for making something significant out of your life."

She laughs without mirth. "The good Dr Cholmondeley was right, by the way, Huck. Warneford is now a hospital. Though when it first opened in 1826 it was known as the Oxford Lunatic Asylum. You don't have to be mad to live here—but it helps!"

As her laughter echoes across the rooftops, I think I glimpse the outline of another person behind her in the darkness of the archway. Moving without sound, the squat figure steps forward, arm raised. "Well," Dr Cholmondeley says, her hand on Kat's shoulder, "it is nice to be right about something."

A puzzled expression forms on Kat's face as she reaches up to her neck, from which Dr Cholmondeley has removed a hypodermic needle.

"Why, Dr Cholmondeley," Kat begins, but the knife in her hand is wavering, "how good of you to join us." The blade drops to the ground and she looks at her empty hands, then at me. "I'm sorry, Huck. What was I saying? You know I was kidding about you jumping—you know that, right?" She takes half a step forward, then half-collapses against the archway. She's gazing at me, her green eyes moist and maybe even sincere. "All I wanted was to have something true, between us and only us." Her words are slurring now. "Because if two people believe a story is true—if they truly *believe* in it—then it may as well be true, right? Isn't that what love is?"

I start to reply, but her eyes are closing. "Can we," she is still speaking, "can we still go to New York together?" Her voice is a whisper now. "If I can make it there, I'll make it anywhere. It's up to you, New York, New..."

For the first time, I see Kat's eyebrows—raised so often sardonically, or framing a rolling of her eyes—relax and soften, her face losing its hardness as it yields to the vulnerability of sleep. Her body slumps and Dr Cholmondeley catches her under the arms, laying her gently on the ground.

"Are you all right up here?" She looks at Mei and myself, her deadpan voice the only sound.

"Yes, I think so," I say.

"I hate to use drugs like this." She shakes her head, putting the container with the needle in the pocket of her coat. "Poor Kat has been in a terrible place ever since her parents died. No child should have to go through what she experienced." She wraps the knife in her scarf and tucks it into her belt.

"Kat told us about it," I say. "It must have been terrible, watching your childhood burn up in flames." Seeing Mei's puzzled expression, I add, "It was some kind of electrical fault. Maybe she joked about it as a way to deal with the pain."

"Electrical fault?" Dr Cholmondeley repeats, crossing Kat's arms over her chest. "The coroner concluded that she was playing with her father's cigarette lighter and a fire got out of control." Her eyes narrow as I produce the silver object from my pocket. "That lighter." I extend my hand and she takes it from me.

"Kat was only a child," she continues, "so there was no question of punishment. I doubt that she wanted to harm her parents." The lighter disappears into her coat alongside the hypodermic needle. She stands once more. "As for you"—she looks me up and down—"I see you ignored both my warnings?"

Kat, the tower, my diary, the messages. "I'm sorry, Dr Cholmondeley," is all that I say. "She convinced me—I convinced myself that you were trying to reserve the secrets in this tower. It's crazy, I know."

"Another word we prefer not to use here, but yes, I do know what you mean." She crouches down to smooth the hair from Kat's eyes. "Your mind chose to believe something impossible, because the alternative was unbearable. I think there may be some truth in what you said about consciousness being a story we tell ourselves. Generally, we want that story to be a pleasant one. Everyone embellishes it here and there—the size of the fish we caught, who left whom when a relationship breaks down. For most people, it's an act of gentle deception—a white lie. For you, because of the many gaps in your memory, it became an act to preserve your sanity."

She looked down at the peaceful face by her feet. "It's not uncommon in such cases to put more stake in the views of those close to us, those we trust emotionally. When you started forming a bond with Kat, you began to believe—you wanted to believe—the things she told you. Because even if you followed her down a rabbit hole, at least you would be together."

"And did I—" I begin. "What happened to Mrs Sellwood?"

Dr Cholmondeley looks at me. "You don't remember any of it?" I shake my head. "It's true that she was stabbed, but not by a patient. She was robbed outside her clinic. Someone tried to steal her bag. It had copies of some patient files she had taken home, so she fought back. I understand that it was you that found her. You tried to stop the bleeding until the medics arrived. There was nothing more you could have done, but she died in your arms. I'm sorry, Huck."

The wind has picked up. A new chill encircles my neck like an icy scarf.

"The first time we spoke properly," Dr Cholmondeley's voice fills the silence, "you showed me a letter she wrote to you. You said that it gave you some comfort in times of darkness." The blank look on my face must show that I don't know what she's talking about. "You said you kept it inside your diary, to remember her?"

I pick up the green volume from the ground. The stitching has been damaged by the fight with Kat, but the other pages seem secure. Delicately, I open it to the middle and restore the sodden piece from the ledge. There is no letter.

"That's odd," Dr Cholmondeley says. "You seemed quite attached to it."

Mei has moved to stand next to Kat and now squats down. Before Dr Cholmondeley can stop her, she goes through Kat's pockets and produces a small white envelope. Holding it up in the dim light, the single word "Huck" is visible in a flowery hand. "I'm guessing she didn't want you to have this," Mei says, passing it to me.

I open the sheet of paper inside. The handwritten note in the same looping script is uncanny—new and yet familiar, like being told about a dream from which you just woke.

Dear Huck,

For a therapist used to talking for a living, writing this down feels a little odd. Yet, as you and I have established, it is the best way to fix a memory for you, to help you ground yourself in something real.

You are a remarkable young man, Huck. You have wit, intelligence, creativity. You have the potential to do great things, and I look forward to cheering you on when you do.

What you don't have is a good memory. Since the car crash, your memories have been scrambled. This affects events in the past, like the accident itself. That's a problem, because your father can't forgive himself for what happened—and, since you don't remember it, you can't forgive him either.

But the crash also impaired your ability to store new memories. Here your wit, intelligence, and creativity work against you, because your brain fills in the gaps that your memory leaves out.

For some years now, we've been using diaries to make up for that. I wanted you to use them as a tool, but I worry that they've become a crutch. My mother used to say that wisdom is the compliment that experience pays to failure. Well, Huck, I'm afraid I've failed you.

As you know, however, we learn more from our mistakes than from our successes. The problem is that a life—your life—is more than events and facts. It's more than a series of diary entries. A life is a story. It has a beginning, a middle, and an end. And, like any story, a good life has meaning, a purpose to it.

So that's my challenge to you, Huck. To make your life more than the sum of its parts, to come up with a story that is more than one fact after another.

If I'm lucky, I'll be around for you to tell it to me one day. But, even if I'm not, I know that you will find someone else with whom you can share it.

Godspeed, Huckleberry. And good luck.

Yours sincerely,
Patricia Sellwood

I refold the letter and put it back in my diary, toward the end. I turn to Dr Cholmondeley, but heavy footsteps are coming up the stairs. The silence of her arrival contrasts with the reverberations as Tshombe emerges from the archway. Above us, the rain has stopped and the moon peaks out from behind a cloud.

"You're OK!" I exclaim.

"Of course, I am OK," he pants, sweating a bit more than seems natural given the coldness of the night. "Though I note that, to get here, I had to brave the dark and some considerable heights." He is wearing a new shirt, but a hint of red stains his neck. He stands next to where Kat lies, staying as far from the edge of the balcony as possible. "What happened to her?"

I explain that she has been sedated and he nods. "It's probably for the best. She is a few sandwiches short of a picnic, that one." Then he takes out his phone for a selfie with the view from the tower. "As for me, father will be very proud."

"He should be, Tshombe," Dr Cholmondeley says. "You have made great strides during your time here. And I, for one, look forward to seeing your drama therapy group perform *Hamlet.*"

"I gather I've already seen some of it?" I add.

"Yes, I am sorry about that." He puts the phone back in his jacket. "Kat bet me that I could not fool you with the death scene. She asked me to play dead, covered in stage blood, then we would all have a good laugh about it. I apologise if it was distressing to you. I let my vanity as an actor overwhelm my considerations as a friend." Looking down at Kat's supine body, he sighs. "I went to the common room afterward. When you did not turn up or answer your phone, I became concerned. That was when I found that Mei had come back. Later, I saw the good doctor here hastening toward the tower."

I take out my phone and switch it off silent mode, seeing the string of missed calls and messages from Tshombe and Mei. And Mom. I quickly send a text that I'm looking forward to seeing her and Dad in time for Christmas. We have a lot to talk about.

There's so much that I still do not understand. "So, which of you was sending me the notes?" I ask.

"What notes?" Dr Cholmondeley says.

"Notes made up of letters cut from the newspaper—like an old-fashioned ransom message. Warning me about Kat and the tower."

This is greeted with blank stares, until Mei breaks the silence. "Is it possible that Kat sent them to you?"

After tonight, I don't feel confident dismissing anything

as impossible. “Well, someone was slipping them under my door. Putting a container full of extra letters in my closet crossed the line from weird to creepy.”

“What did the notes say?” Mei asks.

I remember that they are still in my pocket. “I have them here,” I say, unfolding the pages. “The first said: ‘Be careful, she only lies.’ Then ‘About the Tower, do not believe.’ The third was ‘The sword is worth dying for.’ That does start to sound like Kat. And then tonight I found the note saying ‘Give Kat hope, she deserves it.’ That was what led me to her room tonight.”

Mei reaches for the four sheets of paper. “May I?” She looks at them closely in the moonlight, then folds them so that each of the short messages can be seen together. “We used to get puzzles like this at school. What if they aren’t four messages, but a single message broken into four parts? If you read them in order, it becomes: ‘Be careful. She only lies about the Tower. Do not believe the sword is worth dying. Forgive Kat. Hope she deserves it.’”

“Huck,” Dr Cholmondeley says, “maybe the messages weren’t from Kat. It’s not uncommon for people suffering from memory problems to leave notes for themselves. Much as your diary helps reinforce memories, some people leave reminders for everything from daily tasks to the names of their children—reminders that they forget even writing.”

“You think I wrote this message to myself? Cutting up newspapers so I didn’t recognise my own handwriting?” Not to mention sending it in four parts, making sense only at the end. I wonder.

"I don't know," she confesses. "Yet, to borrow your own phrase, it would hardly be the craziest thing that happened tonight." She looks up as clouds start to cover the moon once again. Not far from the tower, a truck starts its engine. "I think that might be about enough excitement for the evening. I should probably ask an orderly to do this, but I would prefer not to leave Kat in the open. Tshombe, would you be so kind as to help me carry her down the stairs?"

"Certainly," he says, bending down to lift Kat as Dr Cholmondeley cradles her head, smoothing the hair from her eyes. It is the most peaceful I have ever seen Kat. The temptation to kiss her forehead rises. I resist it.

"Can you, Huck?" It takes a second to realise that Dr Cholmondeley is speaking to me.

"What?"

"Can you forgive her?"

I think, before answering with the truth. "I don't know."

As Tshombe and Dr Cholmondeley slowly descend the stairs, the sound of the truck deepens, a throaty roar echoing through the night. I only now notice that the Christmas carollers have stopped singing. Looking down from the tower, I see the truck rumbling along a service lane that runs along the back of Warneford, engine straining. A large tarpaulin covers its bulky load; an angular figure stands watch over its departure. Between movements, the figure is so still as to be unnerving.

"Dr Cholmondeley," I call out as she and Tshombe turn the first corner. "What's with the truck?"

"Nothing that need concern you," she replies over her

shoulder, checking that we are following her while holding Kat's head.

Below us, I see the angular figure fold itself into a silver Aston Martin, its engine a low growl as it follows the truck down the service lane and onto the road to London.

As Dr Cholmondeley and Tshombe turn another corner, Mei hands me back the four notes. We are alone on the balcony, the moon continuing to play hide-and-seek behind the clouds.

"So that's your diary?" She nods at the green leather-bound journal in my hand.

"Yes," I say, rubbing the cover dry on my sweater. Out of habit, I flick toward the end to see how many blank pages are left. Only a couple, but that should be enough.

"So, what happens now?" Mei asks.

I look out at the view across Oxford one last time. "We get on with things. Confront our fears. Live."

We go through the archway and begin the walk down. Passing the clock mechanism, Mei checks the time on her phone. "Eight minutes past eight in the evening exactly," she observes. "What are the chances?"

I shine my own phone's flashlight at the cogs and wheels. They have been cleaned and oiled since I first climbed up here with Kat, glistening in the artificial light. The pendulum hangs still, but it is within arm's reach. I reach out and give it a gentle push, setting into motion the complex set of gears and weights arrayed before us. The pendulum swings back and there is a satisfying tick as the minute hand moves imperceptibly on its renewed circumnavigation of the clock face.

In the darkness, Mei takes my arm. “So,” she says, “do you think you can explain to me what happened here? Starting from the beginning?”

“I can try,” I say. “But is it all right if we don’t begin at the beginning? To make sense of things, to really understand, you sometimes have to start at the end.”

“And what if it’s not the end?”

I pause to consider this. “Then, I guess the story keeps on going—one page at a time.”

The pendulum swings easily now. We watch it for a few more beats then turn our backs on the clock, continuing down into the tower and the courtyard below.

Acknowledgements

Thanks, first and most, to my loving critics M, V, N, and now T. I'm grateful to all those who read versions of the text, in particular Nelle Chesterman, Viv Chesterman, Jen Clay, Kenji Gwee, Shelagh Mahbubani, Judy Sternlight, and Ming Tan. Sebastian Einsiedel corrected my German. Thanks to my wonderful agent, Victoria Skurnick, and the team at Marshall Cavendish—in particular Anita Teo for seeing the book's potential and She-reen Wong for polishing its prose. I also benefited from discussions over the years with individuals at Oxford's Department of Experimental Psychology (which does not run a winter programme) and Singapore's Institute of Mental Health. If the novel has merit, much can be attributed to their combined influence; deficiencies, of course, are mine alone.

About the Author

Educated in Melbourne, Beijing, and Oxford, Simon Chesterman lived briefly in Tanzania and Serbia before moving to New York for six years and finally settling in Singapore. He has written or edited nineteen non-fiction books and is the author most recently of a young adult trilogy—*Raising Arcadia, Finding Arcadia,* and *Being Arcadia*—as well as its companion volume *Codes, Puzzles & Conundrums.*

www.SimonChesterman.com